BARRED
souls

Barred Souls
Pandemonium 1 & 2
By Meredith Katz

Published by Less Than Three Press LLC

All rights reserved. No part of this book may be used or reproduced in any manner without written permission of the publisher, except for the purpose of reviews.

Edited by Amanda Jean
Cover designed by Natasha Snow

This book is a work of fiction and all names, characters, places, and incidents are fictional or used fictitiously. Any resemblance to actual people, places, or events is coincidental.

First Edition February 2017
Copyright © 2017 by Meredith Katz
Printed in the United States of America

Digital ISBN 9781620049488
Print ISBN 9781620049754

For Sam, for whom I made Bru at least 20% more of a hot mess. Happy Valentine's Day, baby.

BARRED
souls

PANDEMONIUM 1 & 2

MEREDITH KATZ

Table of Contents

The Cobbler's Soleless Son 9

Behind Bars 67

THE COBBLER'S *soleless* SON

Renart Walker, the cobbler's son, tilted his head up and breathed in the scent of demons. There were always at least a couple in this town—passing through, hunting, going about their business. Today, though, they crowded into the streets, rubbing shoulders and other parts (not all of them even *had* shoulders) with the humans around them.

Hrahez, the Demon Prince who ruled the fiefdom of which Potfeld was a part, held grand events twice a year. Of these, the humans were only invited to one, and the demons brought the party to *them*.

This year it was a parade, though as always, some kind of celebration had formed around it. Fresh food was being hawked to curious onlookers, and demons turned out to mingle with the crowds, joining in the revelry as it passed through the fief. The purpose, as Renart understood it, was for the prince to show himself off to his fiefdom—to remind them of his presence.

The previous year, it had been a festival and market, though Renart hadn't seen much of it. Right at the start, he'd hooked up with a demon and missed most of the day's events. It wouldn't be the first festival he'd missed like that, though—and he rather hoped it wouldn't be the last.

He wondered vaguely if Tarigan were around this year and what Renart would say to them if so. He didn't think it'd be something he'd have to deal with, even if they were somehow still in Potfeld, Tari probably wouldn't look anything like Renart remembered.

Tari was a cubant—a sex demon. Renart had met incubi and succubi before, cubants manifesting male or female, but Tari was the first intercubus he'd seen. He'd known all cubants could change their bodies' entire appearance at whim, and swapped terms when they did, but wasn't sure if that changed how they thought of themselves.

"Well," Tari had said when Renart had asked, "we're all cubants however we look. *That's* how we identify, kiddo. Pronouns, terms... for some people, demons and humans alike, they definitely matter! But for cubants—and a lot of shapeshifters—they're just descriptions for people who want to put words to *others*. And they help us get what we want." They had paused then, and grinned at Renart. "And I do like getting what I want from you. But we're everything, and we flow back and forth over that range. Male, female, both, in between, outside. We change what we look like and call ourselves to reflect how we feel at the time, though of course some of us have our preferences. But if I start feeling like I want to wear a different shape, I'll use different words."

So that had answered that, and Tari spent a lot of time answering other things besides, some without words entirely. It had been an enjoyable and educational few months, but after that they'd started coming to his window a lot less. When asked, they'd outright admitted they were getting bored of Potfeld, and ruffled his hair as if to take the sting away. Renart had taken that silent apology to mean that they were also bored of *Renart*, and wasn't terribly shocked when one day, Tari just stopped coming around. The two of them hadn't had many interests in common, and Renart's eagerness to learn only got them so far.

Besides, newly of age as he had been, Renart was curious about meeting a *lot* of types of demons at that time, and the way Tari drained his energy made it difficult to play around.

The break-up had set his friends' minds at ease, at least, though Renart carefully avoided telling them that it wasn't stopping him from seeing *other* demons. Most people worried quite a bit about anyone who wanted to hang around with demons. Demons were predators, after all—and humans just their prey, the cities their herds.

Demons didn't hunt humans to death in Hrahez's fiefdom—at least, not so often that it was notable, not if they stayed safely within the cities. Hrahez was rare in that he managed to maintain some sort of balance between giving demons the run of the place and keeping humans relatively safe. He allowed humans to live their lives with minimal interference besides what people brought on themselves—unlike most demon-run fiefdoms, which tended toward tyrannical slavery at best. For the people in *those*, there was never any safety. Fleeing to the few remaining human-run cities wasn't an option either. They rarely let in outsiders, and as he'd heard it, they spent all their time under constant vigilance to *keep* their cities demon-free, with citizens reporting each other for interrogation at the slightest hint of anything that could have been attributed to demonic influence.

Of course, people complained about Hrahez anyway, but it didn't sound to Renart like things were terribly different overall from the centuries before the demons had appeared. One way or another there'd be an aristocracy with a common class to serve their needs. Whether it was humans preying on humans or demons doing it instead, Renart couldn't see the point in trying to draw a distinction.

At least the demons were *interesting*.

Music rang out suddenly, signaling the start of the procession. Renart was torn from his thoughts by his excitement, pushing himself up on the balls of his feet to try to see over the crowd.

He knew Hrahez would be leading the way, but even if he hadn't known, there would have been no doubt which one of the demons was the prince. He was riding a black horse that didn't quite move like a horse, limbs flowing too smoothly, eyes so shadowed in its dark face that Renart couldn't really say for sure that it even had them. Hrahez's robes were draped over both himself and his horse so that he seemed to become part of the creature, sleek black hair so long that it melded in as well, flowing behind him like a cape. His curled horns weighed his head back so his chin was held high.

Renart's breath caught.

He had known Hrahez was an incubus, but hadn't anticipated the sheer aura he had. He exuded charisma, charm, *desire*. It washed over Renart with such intensity that he thought he might die, *wanted* to be crushed by that sensation more than he'd ever wanted anything. He sighed with an involuntary, sudden longing and heard the rest of the crowd do so as well, a loud exhalation from all around.

There was no reason for Renart to stand out in that mass of meaningless faces and sounds, he knew. He was near the front but not quite at it, and wasn't tall enough to catch anyone's attention in a crowd.

Despite that, their eyes met.

A memory washed over Renart, visceral, of being a child, lying on his back in the fields outside the dubious protection of Potfeld's walls. He'd been staring up at the wide black sky with its million points of light, breathing in the cool fall air, shivering and waiting. At the time, he'd felt very small and alone in the darkness, and liked it that way. He stayed out very late, as late as he could without starting to drowse, and wondered if a monster might come and eat him. When one didn't, he finally went back home, disappointed. He'd climbed up to his window to sneak back in, his mother none the wiser, and felt a little lonely, lacking something he couldn't name.

The bright flecks of gold in Hrahez's forest-green eyes were like stars. Looking into them made Renart long for it again—that sky, that hypothetical monster. He wanted to be devoured, and to fight back from the inside. As an adult, it sank into him in a new way.

They didn't speak to each other. They couldn't have even if they'd wanted to, separated by the crowd, Hrahez leading a procession that wouldn't stop. Their gaze held as Hrahez rode past, and was broken only when the prince would have to crane his neck to keep it.

Renart watched Hrahez's back until it too was out of sight, and then couldn't seem to focus on the parade itself. The crowd was shifting and talking, excitement and fear, and he felt a rush of sudden irritation.

The person next to him nudged him. "Did you see him look at the crowd? Gave me chills. I swear he was looking right at me!"

No question who the girl meant, though he felt a

little offended at her assumption. "I saw," he said. "I wanted..." He didn't know how he could end that, and didn't bother trying. Not much of a point telling a stranger about that feeling, that desire to throw himself to the wolves just to see if they'd want to eat him.

The girl made a face. "Of course you wanted him! He's an incubus. I want him too... Oh, I swear my legs are weak..."

Renart's stomach twisted with his annoyance. He couldn't enjoy the parade, not any more. After Hrahez, everything else seemed like a cheap performance.

"I have to go," he said.

~~*

When Renart returned home that night, his mother seized him by the ear and began dragging him over to her work desk. "I cannot believe you," she sighed. "Going out to the yearly festival like you're some kind of damn child? You're a man of nineteen, and it's high time you acted it!"

"Ow, ow! Mum, you know these festivals aren't for chil—"

"You've work to do, lad," she said, and took her seat again, handing him her cobbler's last and an insole. He obligingly began to press the last down against the insole, taking the sections of leather as she passed them over and placing them so she could tack the parts together. "Yes, argue back, certainly. Oh, you're clever all right, but what good is that when you can't help in the shop on a day like today? Do you know how much business we've been getting?"

He managed to keep from rolling his eyes through

force of will. Obviously, it had been a hectic day for her. "I'm helping right now, mum."

She eyed him dourly, but accepted that. "Not a thought of duty in your mind," she muttered, pressing a tack down and hammering it into place. "Always chasing your dreams. You should count yourself lucky, you know. If we lived in any other fiefdom, you wouldn't get to go out and play with those *demons*. They'd have you out working in the quarries or the fields—"

"Or the mines," he agreed affably. "Toiling away in misery at a job I didn't choose nor wished anything to do with. What a fate that would be!"

Her hammer landed heavily on her bench. "Now listen here, Renart. You *should* be the future cobbler one day, but you don't act like you intend for that to happen. Nor do you look into any other work—you just faff around all day! It's time for you to focus, because I'm not getting any younger. I don't want to hire myself an apprentice, not when you already have this kind of skill."

"I've been learning from the best, mum," he said with a winning smile and an utter lack of interest. He'd been watching his mother day in and day out since he was a child. *She* could pour her wants into the leather, shape it and change it and be satisfied when the end result was a boot. But leather was a tool, and it would only ever change as it was forced to. There was no challenge in it for him.

"Hold it *steady*, Renart!"

"Yes, mum," he said, and let his mind wander as she continued to grumble.

Now, Prince Hrahez... that'd be a challenge. Completely out of his reach, of course. Most of the time when he went after a demon, he'd just walk up and introduce himself—but there was no way he'd just see Hrahez passing by casually on the town's streets like he did any other demon. He couldn't just go looking for him, either. There was no way for him to know where Hrahez was at any given time beyond the events he held.

Waiting a full year to catch a glimpse of him again would be agonizing.

Even if he got lucky and did, somehow, just *happen* to see Hrahez around, it wouldn't work out. He was sure of that. It was already difficult to make it so he was treated seriously by any of the demons he'd approached, but a *prince?* Renart needed to do something to get his attention, or he'd be beneath his notice. At best, he'd be used and thrown away. At worst, he'd be used right up. That had its own appeal, but sounded awfully temporary.

There had to be something he could do. Some way to be acknowledged.

But he couldn't think of anything.

~~*

Months passed, and it felt like his mind was always working. Whenever he wasn't distracted, he was thinking of *opportunities*. Making plans, discarding them, and starting all over again. His mother praised him for how devoted he was to business these days, but it was just easier to think when his hands were busy.

Renart was mulling it over one late summer day, sitting out front of the shop and working some leather, and almost scraped himself with his tool when he was hit by a wave of desire. He looked up, knowing he'd see a cubant, hoping absurdly that it might actually be Prince Hrahez.

It was a succubus, and she was beautiful. Voluptuous and fleshy, she was entirely made out of curves: round thighs and round hips, round waist and round breasts, curly hair bouncing with every step she took. She was tall too, he noticed. Her horns—two slick things that pointed up like reflective crescent moons—only made her taller. There was just a *lot* of her.

The succubus glanced his way as his head jerked up toward her, and she smirked as their eyes met. Arousal washed over him again, but along with it—with *finally* seeing a demon around again who'd bothered to even look his way—came an idea. It was a half-formed plan, poorly-thought-out at best, but he didn't have the *time* to think it through properly. She was on her way somewhere, and if he didn't say anything, she'd continue on. He smiled back, knowing that what he was about to do was probably pure suicide. The risk was heady. A little excited, he rose to his feet.

"Lady demon," he said. "A moment of your time?"

For a moment, he thought she'd consider him beneath her regard—that she'd keep walking on without hesitation. Her gold-flecked green eyes returned to the road briefly before meeting his again, but she *did* stop, and spread her arms with a shrug. *You got my attention; now what?* her posture said. "I hope it will take more than a moment," she said aloud, lips still curved.

His heart was beating fast, heat flushing his body, the weight of arousal growing in him. It settled heavily around his throat, his chest, his groin. She was affecting him, and even without the vague plan slowly coming together, he wanted her. He flashed her a grin, running fingers through his hair. "I'm counting on it," he said.

The succubus lifted a brow at the surety, smiling back, then offered a hand to him. "Well, then?"

Renart took it, and led her from the porch around the building, taking the back way into the shop. He needed to get the succubus up to his room on the second floor, but his mother would be on the shop floor, working and selling. There was no way he wanted to cross her line of sight, not while sneaking a demon inside. Sure enough, the path was clear from the back door, and he grasped the demon's hand in his own slightly sweaty one, almost dragging her up the steps to his room.

She let out a laugh, amused and startled. "Eager, aren't we?"

"You have no idea," he said. She could smell and taste the arousal rolling off him, he knew that much. Tari had described it to him once. It was, they'd said, similar to how smelling food made you hungrier, and sometimes even made you start to taste it already.

The succubus probably had *some* idea how eager he was, he thought ruefully. Even if she herself weren't so appealing, the danger of his plan would have got his blood pumping.

They didn't waste any time going about it, barely undressing. He was already hard, and she was ready for him. As soon as the door was shut she was on him, slamming him back against it hard enough that he saw stars. His feet scrabbled on the ground to brace himself as she sank down to her knees, unfastened his pants, and drew his cock out.

Her eyes glittered up at him and her mouth opened, small fangs outlining a broad wet tongue. Eager, wanting, *elated*, he grabbed her horns to hold on as she swallowed him down.

The horns didn't give him any control, for better or worse—they were just something to ground himself to. She was stronger than he was, and nothing he could do would affect her movements. Her head bobbed as she took him in over and over, mouth working, tongue lashing, one hand squeezing his balls, her other one stroking down her own body to settle between her legs. At least by holding her horns he could find himself again in that whirlwind of pleasure, have a sense that he still existed. He gripped them, white-knuckled as he ground his hips forward to push himself into the hungry warmth of her mouth, thrusting hard and fast. No need to worry about her throat. Cubants designed their bodies around things like this and he felt no resistance, no strain, as she moved on him.

Renart reached the edge fast, but she didn't let him come easily, grabbing tight around the base and leaning away from him to draw in a breath. It almost hurt when her mouth left him. He was so close, so eager, wanted it so badly. He *ached* for that moment when he could feel her drink a fragment of his spirit down, swallowing his life out of himself and leaving him a little emptier than before. It was absolutely addictive. The risk was the best part of sleeping with demons, he'd found, *especially* with cubants.

Before he could do more than voice a whine, she grinned up at him, licked her lips, and carefully tossed him across the room from his door to the bed. His own breath went out in a rush, the shock of slamming into his bed pushing him away from the edge of orgasm slightly, though he nearly came anyway when she began crawling over him. Her breasts had spilled from the straps of her shirt and her skirt was hiked up to her waist, leaving her clothes framing her body rather than covering it. He reached up to pull her down, wrapped his arms around her and held on as she sank down on top of him, pulling him inside her.

Renart couldn't hear anything beyond his gasps, his struggles to breathe, the wet sounds of their bodies moving against each other. He couldn't focus at all. If she wanted to kill him, she could. The pleasure was too hot, her insides pulling at him, and all through it, her eyes stayed on his, staring as she sucked at his life force, pulling him in, pulling him in, *pulling him in*—

He came with a shocking intensity, shuddering through the pleasure as it peaked nearly to pain. It lasted just a moment too long, agonizing, then slowly ebbed, leaving him panting as he sank back against the bed. The room swam in front of him but he was still awake, at least, and he had his own mind about him. Good; he hadn't been sure he would.

That was always a risk.

The demon had begun to pull away. Hastily, he grabbed the strap of her outfit under her arm before she could go far. "Wait," he managed, tongue thick in his mouth. "Please."

"Hm?" She settled back on the bed, leaning over him. "Not enough? You're playing a dangerous game, boy."

"Not that," he said, and smiled at her with enough genuine fondness—if not for her specifically, for her *kind*—that she seemed taken aback. He hadn't even begun to play his dangerous game yet. "I want to talk about something. Make... a deal."

"A deal?" She lifted her brows, pulling her strappy outfit back into something resembling the right place. The playfulness had vanished from her eyes, leaving behind a curiosity and hardness. The hair on his arms raised in a sudden chill as she considered his request. "What sort of thing are you looking for? You know I won't go easy on you just because we've had a moment."

"I'm not expecting you to," he assured her quickly. He could slowly feel his wits coming together properly again, mind recovering in the aftermath of his lust, starting to get back what felt like proper control over human speech. He smiled again, half to test out how his mouth felt. "I'll set proper terms, don't worry."

The demon reclined beside him on the bed, tail curling over one leg. She reached over to push Renart's floppy hair out of his eyes with too-long fingers. The brush of fingers on his forehead almost seemed to burn, a vague spike of arousal starting to stir again. The act was playful but the look in her eyes was thoughtful and a little scornful, and he tried not to show that he'd noticed. "What do you want, then?" she asked.

He took the time to breathe deeply and focus. He couldn't afford to mess this up, or he'd really be the fool she clearly thought he was. "I want to meet Prince Hrahez," he said. "And for that, I'll give you all the soul I have in my possession right now."

She blinked, her horizontal pupils narrowing as they focused on him, and then let out a startled laugh. "What sort of turn of phrase is that? Do you think maybe I'd just take part of your soul, perhaps your passion for life or your love of dancing? Or have you perhaps sold off part of your soul, or loaned it out?"

"No," he said, and willed his heart to calm down and beat steadily. "I just wanted to be specific."

She watched him for a moment, inscrutable, then exhaled, her smile curving again into something almost fond, a little reluctant. "You really shouldn't bother making a deal like this," she said gently. "You don't know Prince Hrahez, and anyway, he's an incubus. Even if you became the prince's lover, you'll hardly have his sole attention. Humans often want that, right? But it's not possible. You know we steal the life-force of our lovers; if the prince agreed to monogamy, you'd die quickly enough."

Renart shook his head, sitting up properly next to her, legs crossed. It wasn't the most dignified position, naked as he was, but he figured she'd seen it all before. He leaned over and grinned at her. "I don't care," he said. "I've dated a cubant before and haven't minded. He can have as many lovers on the side as he wants if he's mine regardless."

That drew another laugh from her. "The prince yours, rather than you the prince's? I can get you to meet him, but I can't promise *that*."

"I know," he said. "Anyway, you're right that I don't know him. But I know he's fair. I've seen how he's been running his fiefdom and I know what the other options are like. He's even said before that if people think he leads them poorly, they're welcome to try to overthrow him."

"A threat or a challenge, not a kindness," she countered.

There wasn't much point arguing it. She knew Hrahez, and Renart didn't. "Could be one," he agreed.

"I've heard that the prince loves a good challenge. That he loves to play games and toy with people." It felt risky, like he was pushing too hard, but he met her eyes again.

Adrenaline hummed through him, and he couldn't keep from smiling from the thrill. The expression felt a bit weird, not quite right on his face. "But I do too," he continued. "If he meant that as a challenge, then he still wants someone to try him. He's above threatening for the sake of it, but he dared them regardless. I want to challenge him back—though of course I don't want to overthrow him. But I don't know how I would meet him. I can't get into any of the events where I actually could talk to him. You know that humans aren't allowed to those."

Her own smile had faded slowly as she watched him, listened to him talk. More than anything, she looked intrigued. "It's to protect them. The demons at those parties would eat any wandering humans right up."

"I'm sure!" Renart said, nodding, his tone light. "If a human's not invited, nothing to stop a demon from taking advantage of that intrusion. See, what a nice guy, protecting his people from his own kind!" Her arguments didn't matter to him, and he wished she'd stop making them. He didn't care what the reason was. It was just one more barrier to him actually getting there—and *that* was all that mattered. "Why do you care so much? *You're* not going to lose out if this deal goes badly for me. You'll have what you want either way. That's what's important, right? So don't hesitate." He stuck out a hand.

His heart was in his throat. If she refused this, if she thought he was trying to play her, it'd all be for nothing. If she got the best of him... *I'd never get to meet Hrahez*, he thought wistfully, and looked at her hand instead of her face, afraid she could read it in him.

Finally she sighed again, almost put-upon. "Oh, very well," she said, and took his hand. "I'll get you an invitation to meet the prince at one of his soirees, as you wish, for all the soul you have in your possession."

He shook it, feeling the heady rush of elation, of victory—and then reached down, leaning over the edge of the bed, picking up his shoes. He snagged a prying tool from nearby with a quick sweep of his hand, then sat up with both. His heart was pounding so hard that he thought it might come right out, giddy.

I've done it.

It took barely any effort at all to hook the edge of the sole and begin to work it free.

She made an audible choking noise. "—*Really?*"

"Verbal agreement. I was really going to be in trouble if you wrote it down, but I thought if I put my hand out first," he explained as the first sole came off, "it might work." Relief had made him almost shaky, voice trembling.

Renart was fairly sure, from her initial amused disbelief, that he wasn't going to be in trouble. He *knew* he had her when her slitted eyes narrowed, head falling back as she let out a genuine guffaw.

"Fine, you're right," she said, wiping a tear away with one finger. "I shouldn't have made a verbal bargain! I ignored the basics—mistaking you for an illiterate fool was *my* mistake. I'll take these, then."

He finished prying off the second sole and handed them both to her. "You can't have any of the other soles in the building," he told her. "The ones that have sold belong to their buyers, and the ones that haven't are still my mother's. She's the cobbler; I'm only her son."

"Fair enough." She took the pair of shoe soles, dangling them between her fingertips, and her pupils dilated again. Her smile tightened and her voice dropped. "Don't think you can get out of this so easily by just offering me two strips of leather, however."

Renart nodded. He'd accepted that she'd do some form of push back when he came up with the idea. There was nothing to do but accept it. "What is it, then?"

Her gaze felt like it was boring into him; he couldn't blink even if he wanted to, his dry eyes stinging. Power had gathered around her. She said softly, "You have two more soles in your possession. The bottoms of your feet belong to me now as well. But rather than cutting those off you, I'm setting conditions."

Even trying to answer, his voice wouldn't come.

She held up a finger and his eyes jerked to it. "You've given away your soles, so the bottoms of your feet aren't yours to clothe any longer. You will never be able to wear shoes that have a sole to them. The moment you put them on, they'll fall apart. You'll be the cobbler's soleless son. Eventually, you may become the soleless cobbler, and I wonder how you'll sell shoes at all if you're apparently unwilling to wear them."

He found his voice again in a rush as she released the pressure on him just a little. His eyes were watering from his need to blink, sending tears down his cheek. "That's fine," he managed.

"Is it? I wonder," she said, and sighed. Suddenly, the tension broke as she looked down and away. He blinked rapidly, scrubbing at his eyes with the heels of his palms. When he'd managed to clear them enough to look up, she was holding a card out to him.

"This is—"

"The invitation you wanted," she said, and suddenly she was smiling again, almost pleased with herself. "Prince Hrahez is throwing a grand party for demons, as you expected. No humans are allowed, but with this, you'll be an exception. It's two months away, so I hope you'll be prepared by then."

Swallowing, Renart reached out and took it. The invitation felt soft in his hands, more silk than paper. He opened it and looked it over, trying to confirm that everything was in order, but the writing in it wasn't readable, a foreign script crawling across the page as he tried to focus on it. For all he knew, it was like that old wives' tale of demons who sent human messengers to each other as prey. *This is the last one for today. Eat up.* All he could do was trust her, though, and the deal she made with him—as much as he'd taken advantage of it.

"Be careful," she told him, and then reached over and patted his head. "You're right that he's put out edicts for us to live in harmony with his human citizens, but you'll find it's different being a human out of the city, in *our* territory."

And with that, she was gone. He didn't see her leave, but she was no longer there. The window was open, and his curtain blew softly in the afternoon breeze. From below, he could hear his mother calling for him.

He ignored her. He *had* to experiment.

He searched around, found a shoe that he'd been working on for an order, and put it on. His foot pushed right through like the whole thing was made of paper, the sole falling off, tacks sliding out of place and landing on the wood floor, rolling and bouncing around. He'd likely be finding *those* the hard way.

Slowly, he bent down and picked the shoe sole up, looking at it curiously.

"Huh," he said.

~~*

Two months was a long time to wait, and it wasn't as if Renart could hide his new situation from his mother. He tried acting as if he wasn't wearing shoes because he was, as he'd told her lightly, "rebellious". For a while, he'd thought it was going to work—might even work right up until the party.

But after a week and a half, she shut him in the kitchen while he was eating breakfast. "I've had enough of you going around barefoot," she said sharply. "You're making a mockery of our work, and the whole town's talking about it. I'm putting shoes on you whether you like it or not."

There was no dodging it any longer. He shrugged and said, "I think that won't work." Sitting passively, he let her wrestle the shoe onto his foot. As he'd expected, the nails pinged to the ground without any hesitation, the sole peeling away and falling after.

Another shoe, and another, and she was swearing with increasing inventiveness before she finally glared at him, his ankle firmly in her grip. "Renart Walker, what *have* you done?"

"It's no big deal," he protested, then winced as she gave him the most exasperated, disgusted look he thought he'd ever received in his life. "Look, it's for a good cause."

She groaned, turning her gaze to the heavens as if they could somehow help her. "You've gotten your feet cursed. You've gone and made trouble with a demon and gotten your feet cursed."

He put on a bright and appeasing smile, holding both hands up to her. It was probably better that she believe it to be a curse rather than something he'd done of his own free will. "Something like that," he said agreeably. "I'll figure something out, don't you mind it."

"You're a walking advertisement!" she told him, somewhere between astonishment and outrage. "We both are! The shoes we wear have to stand out. If we wear anything shoddy, we'll lose our clientele, and if we don't wear anything at all... Renart, how come you never think!"

"I think," he protested. "I'm always thinking. Give me three days and I'll come up with something to fix this problem. It'll be grand. Even you won't be able to complain about it, Mum."

She shook her head, sighing. "Three days, and you're not to leave the house until you do."

"*Mum.*"

"My final word!"

That was fair enough, all things considered. He pouted regardless, sweeping a dismal bow to her, then was forced to dart up the stairs to his room as she aimed a swat with the sole of one of the shoes she'd tried to put on him.

It took him half a day to come up with the plan of what he could wear instead of shoes and the full two and a half remaining to get it completed. He worked long hours, wearing his fingers raw with awl and knife, with hot water and dye. He bled as he worked as well, just a little, raw edges of skin pressed to the leather, but that was important as well. He was no magician, but every creator had some essence of magic around them, since magic itself was the ability to transform a concept into a reality. Even if the execution was through hard work only, he pushed what power he could into enchanting the leather, sleeping only when he needed it and taking his dinner in his room.

When he was done, he sat back and looked at it proudly. It really was something impressive, he thought.

Renart had made himself anklets; they wound down the top and sides of his feet and left his soles, by necessity, bare. Soft spirals and patterns wound all over them, mimicking the lacing that would tie them on; those held the core of the magic he'd worked into them, the little he could manage. They were magicked to draw the eye, draw attention, draw *admiration*. If he'd done it well, people would appreciate the craftsmanship even if they thought he was foolish to go around barefoot, they would think, *if the cobbler's son can make that look good with the underside of his damn feet uncovered, what could the cobbler herself make for us in* proper *boots?*

His mother looked less than pleased when he showed them off with an exhausted pride. "I thought you wanted those three days to find a way to break the curse," she said mournfully and somehow resigned, as if she hadn't really expected anything more. "But they'll have to do." As she bent and examined them on him, she relented a little. "They're not half bad, are they? You even put enough of yourself into them to give them a touch of enchantment. If only you put that much effort into all your work, Renart, you'd be in a fine state to take over after me! Where would I even find someone else as talented as you?"

"You'd train them into it, of course," he said, pleased with himself. "Better to have someone with motivation than mere talent, right mum?"

"Get on with you," she said, exasperated, and he was more than happy to immediately comply. It felt like the first time he'd been free in *weeks*, even if it had only been three days, and he popped out the door without bothering to say farewell.

It was good to be out and about with the anklets strapped to his feet. Certainly, his feet still felt nearly as raw as they had since he'd started going barefoot, with stones biting in and grass catching at his soles. But the fresh air felt nice, and he saw people glancing at his legs and whispering. The magic of the anklets was indeed working on more than just his mother. Well, he reminded himself, they could be just reacting to his bare feet by themselves, but he didn't think so. He'd received enough confused looks over those in his first week that he hoped he could tell the difference.

Time went on, and his feet hardened. Not too much, perhaps not *really* enough for a trip, but walking outdoors had become much more endurable. That was important by itself. He wouldn't like to show up at a dance hobbling, after all.

So he went about, training his feet until he was sure he'd be fine on the journey to the manor where the event was to be held.

~~*

When the time came, he told his friends that he might be away for a bit on a chore for his mum, and told his mum that he was going out with his friends for a while. There was a good chance that things would go unsuccessfully out there, and if it did she'd be better off not knowing what had happened to him. If things went well, he could follow up with her at his leisure.

So long as he lived, he was sure he'd find a way to let her know what had happened to him.

The party was to be held at a place not far out of town, a country manor that at other times of the year lay empty. Everyone in the city knew about the event, and everyone knew, too, that they were forbidden to travel there without an invitation. A few would probably go regardless: gossips, storytellers and black market sellers who'd try to get some evidence of the demons' activities one way or another. They'd try to spy in windows—if they got that far—or search the grounds after the fact for any remnants of the demons. Renart had heard from the town's hedge-wizards that scales or horn sheddings were perfectly good spell components, and had occasionally thought of searching his room for some to sell them. He'd never quite bothered, though he was sure he could at least find a hair or two somewhere on his pillow.

Renart put on his best clothes, though he knew they weren't terribly fancy—loose white shirt, violet vest, plain tan culottes and a matching jabot—and fastened his anklets. They didn't quite match and made his bare knees stand out. But still, he thought as he considered himself in front of the mirror, he didn't look half bad. His floppy brown hair was neatly washed and brushed, his dusky skin clean. The time spent on the road would doubtlessly ruin some of the tidiness of his appearance, but there was no point in second-guessing himself now.

He set out, climbing the simple low gate leading out of the city rather than going through the bother of finding someone to unlock it, and walked off down the gravel road. It was immediately uncomfortable, especially compared to the cobbled streets of the city. Sharp stones dug in when he walked on the street itself, but edged grass at the roadside caught at his feet when he tried to walk there instead. Not as bad as it would have been if he hadn't been practicing, he told himself firmly, and continued doggedly onward.

Still, although he was right about how the exercise and heat would make him sweat, he hadn't really anticipated how dirty his feet would get on such a long walk. Dust and mud and dirt clung to them, not something he could just scrape off at the door, not with them bare. It stuck between his toes, caked on and built up as he kept walking. By the time he arrived two hours later, the sun setting and casting his shadow long behind him, he was more than half-tempted to turn right back around. He doubted he'd make a good impression, looking like he meant to bring half the road in with him.

But a bad impression was, he thought, still better than no impression at all. Stealing himself, Renart went up to the door and knocked.

It was opened by a demonic footman, an incubus with long, molten gold hair. Heavy pale lashes half-covered green eyes with light flecks that matched his hair. His horns curved backward like a ram's, wrapping around his head and keeping his hair off his face. Their eyes met, and Renart's heart thudded hard as the footman's aura of desire wrapped around him.

"My goodness," the footman said, in a soft voice. "What have we here?"

Renart drew a sharp breath to center himself, almost undone by the honey scent of the demon in the doorway. With his grip on it a little too tight, he thrust the invitation forward. "I've been invited to this event," he said, mouth dry. "Is there a problem?"

The footman took the invitation, plucking it from Renart's hands with fingers that seemed to have too many joints. He looked it over in a perfunctory way, not even truly bothering to read it, and handed it back. "No problem at all, sir," he said, and curled his lips in a smile. "Except the state of your feet. You'll get mud all over our floors."

"Floors can be cleaned," Renart said, breathless but trying to keep his voice firm. He wasn't sure how hard he'd need to argue to get in, not with the invitation to back him up, but he was determined not to budge.

To his surprise, the footman laughed, shaking his head. "They can, and so can feet," he said, and, unexpectedly, knelt in front of Renart. He ran his fingers down the bare skin of Renart's leg from knee to where the anklets began, then lifted one of Renart's feet, unbalancing him. Suddenly worried he'd fall, Renart braced himself on the wall. "It wouldn't do to show your feet this way in front of the prince."

The touch of those long, unnatural fingers was, Renart was sure, deliberately arousing. Sometimes cubants were so *unfair*. He swallowed hard. "Wouldn't it?" he managed.

"Of course," the footman said. He ran a fingertip over the anklet he was holding. "But my word, you've made something interesting of this embarrassment."

Renart closed his eyes and drew a slow breath. He had to focus. "Then, am I permitted to wash my feet?"

The footman released his leg. "Yes," he said, smiling warmly as he rose again. "Come with me." He took one of Renart's hands, disallowing any argument, then led Renart around the corner of the building.

A large and elaborate garden maze spread out in that direction, and Renart couldn't quite stop his sudden fear. His mind began to run a mile a minute. Perhaps he was being brought out there to be lost in it, left behind so that even his invitation had no value. He'd let himself be taken away from the doorway even when he'd reminded himself to stay firm—he'd put himself at risk. The invitation would hypothetically keep him safe inside the party as a fellow guest, but outside it...

To his relief, the footman released him before they made it to the maze's entrance. He stopped in the small alcove just before the maze proper and began to draw water from a pump.

"Sit," the footman ordered gently. Renart sat on the stone bench, watching the line of the footman's back, the fall of his hair, as he filled a bucket. His admiration didn't go unnoticed, he was sure, and when the footman returned, his horizontally-slitted pupils flicked down the length of Renart's body toward his anklets.

"Take those off," the footman said with a purr, as if he meant more than the anklets. "You wouldn't like them to get wet, I'm sure."

It was impossible to resist. Renart licked his dry lips, leaning down obligingly. His forehead almost brushed the kneeling footman's, their faces close. He breathed in the footman's exhaled breath, a sweet flavor, and unbuckled his anklets.

"Better," the footman murmured. He pulled a cloth out of the bucket and began to run it over Renart's feet. It was almost gentle enough to tickle, but not quite. Instead, it just left him feeling almost agonizingly sensitive, the slow passes of the cloth quickening his breath and hardening his cock.

Renart licked his lips, fingers curling against the bench. He wasn't sure he could bring himself to blink. There shouldn't have been anything erotic about it—wiping his foot, ringing the cloth, soaking it again—but that didn't seem to matter to his body. When one foot was clean and the footman was picking up the other, he couldn't stay silent any more. "Do you give each of your guests this much personal attention?" His voice sounded hoarser than he'd intended, and he felt his cheeks burn.

The footman glanced up at him again, expression warm. "Is that a complaint I hear?" he asked softly, cleaning the other foot.

"No, just..."

"Just nothing, then."

Renart shuddered at the next pass of the footman's fingers. "Just... if you're going to work me up this much... is that the only thing you want to do?"

He was an incubus, after all. There's no way he hadn't noticed Renart's interest.

"Hm." The footman's gaze was still heated, lips curved. He dropped the rag back in the bucket, and slid his fingers up Renart's thighs, making Renart arch with a shock of pleasure.

The footman's fingers caressed slowly up the inside of his legs, then pushed them open. The sudden lack of balance made Renart fall back against the wall behind the bench, breath hitching with lust. He felt shockingly exposed for how clothed he was, and shuddered as the footman passed a hand over his groin.

"I *do* see you're quite worked up," the footman breathed.

"Yes..."

"But I've duties to attend to," the footman said. His expression shifted, warm smile becoming a sudden sharp-edged cruel thing, the pointed tip of his tongue sticking out between his parted lips. "More's the shame. You might as well go in and dance just like that."

"I'll get eaten alive," Renart protested, squirming, trying to sit up properly.

The footman shrugged, keeping him back with a hand on his chest. "It's a risk."

"Won't you help me?" It came out pleadingly, his tone embarrassing, but he couldn't seem to stop it.

"I will not," the footman breathed, his eyes glittering. Despite that, he pressed an open-mouthed kiss to Renart's tented pants, hot breath riling him up more. "Though I do wish you luck in resolving your dilemma."

And with that, the footman rose, drying his hands off perfunctorily on his own black pant legs, and headed back around the side of the house.

Sprawled ungracefully on the bench, Renart let out a soft whine. He'd told the truth, and knew it. *I'm already a lamb to the slaughter just by being a human attending this party.* Going in dazed and aroused was tantamount to suicide.

Wet feet cooling in the evening air, he licked his lips and unbuttoned his pants.

This was a bad idea too. Even if he was alone in the garden for now, there was no guarantee it would stay that way. Plenty of demons fed on sex, and if any were close enough to sense him, he'd be inviting them, and wouldn't necessarily have the liberty of picking his partner. He'd be lucky if it were a cubant, too; there were plenty of other kinds of demons who fed on flesh and fear and pain.

He squirmed in place and sighed, throwing his concerns away. Worrying about it was pointless. Going inside like this was a bigger risk, and waiting for demon-touched arousal to go away on its own might cost him his chance to meet the prince. The only other option was to head home, and there was no way he'd do *that*. He'd taken all these chances so far in order to meet Hrahez—what were a few more?

He'd just have to be quick about it.

Renart closed his eyes, licked his hand, and then curled it around himself. He jacked himself quickly, almost relentlessly, shoving a hand up inside his shirt to tweak a nipple into a hard point. He couldn't stop thinking about how something about this—the scent, the energy of it, whatever—might draw attention, and if anything, that made him harder.

Good, he thought. *Go fast. I'll meet Prince Hrahez.*

He rubbed his wet feet against each other. He remembered the feeling of the footman's hands there, the slow pass of his cloth, and let himself get lost in the visceral memory. He thought of the footman's eyes, the gold shifting in their depths, the way he'd kept gazing up at him. Renart shuddered hard, shoving his hips up as he thrust into his own grip, his shoulders grinding back into the wall behind him.

It didn't take much more than that. He came

quickly and a bit perfunctorily, not very satisfying. He was getting too used to sleeping with demons, he thought wryly, hardly able to hear his own thoughts past the pounding of his heart. Anything less than that inhuman high was starting to feel a bit disappointing.

He couldn't find it in himself to regret that.

Renart wiped himself down with the cloth that the footman had left behind, then cleaned his hands, tucked his cock away and refastened his anklets.

Finally he got up again. His rear was a little cold from being pressed to the stone bench, but he felt good—better than he had before meeting the footman. More confident and less easily distracted by his own excitement and anticipation.

At least he'd managed to take the edge off.

Keeping his head up, he turned the corner of the building again to the entrance. The previous footman was gone, which struck him as a bit odd. Still, even with a new demon to greet him there, he didn't have any trouble. The footman's replacement, a red-skinned and bald-headed giant of a demon, simply read over his invitation and gestured him in.

The ambiance washed over him immediately. Music was playing, though nobody was dancing, as though they were waiting for something. The prince's arrival, perhaps? Nobody was showing any particular obsequiences to any one person, so Hrahez likely wasn't here yet, rather than here and in a shape Renart wouldn't recognize.

Looking around took his breath away, though. He felt stunned by the variety of demons mingling together and filling the room in a mass of sizes, shapes, and colors. They were all over the grand hall, standing together, walking around, flying, hovering near tables, conversing. Some were clothed, but many were not. Some weren't even in shapes that could manage clothes if they tried. A creature largely made of eyes and tentacles wandered past him as he gawked.

I could have anything here. The thought came almost unbidden. He'd seen what he'd thought was a lot of demons, those that showed up to the festival, or those who passed through Potfeld, but there were kinds of demons here he'd never laid eyes on. He wanted to know more, wanted to hear more, knew he probably wouldn't survive doing so but—

But if he got distracted he wouldn't meet Hrahez.

Suddenly the crowd seemed almost absurd, more an obstacle than an appeal. If he wanted to be around demons, becoming Demon Prince Hrahez's lover would grant that, so why get distracted now? It felt almost like a challenge that had been put down for him. *Can you ignore this? Come find me.*

Even as he knew the thought was absurd, he smiled a little to himself. *Of course,* he thought back, filling out the fantasy.

He drew in a slow breath and focused.

The safest bet in surviving to meet the prince was probably in staying near the edges, at least for now. He was already attracting attention by hovering in the doorway. Hurriedly, he walked over to one of the refreshment tables.

He nearly regretted doing so right away. The arms and legs that served for food on the table were clearly of no animal origin, and he averted his eyes, starting to retreat. With a jolt, he ran into someone, and jerked away again, bumping into yet another solid figure in his failed retreat.

"Careful, son." The demon he'd backed into put a

hand on Renart's shoulder to steady him. They were a tall individual of several sexes, and a sort of demon Renart vaguely recalled liked fear. Curling green hair was rolling down to cover their chest, solid-black eyes turned in Renart's direction. "This isn't the safest place for a live one of you."

Renart managed a smile. "I'm starting to realize that," he said. He knew demons, he reminded himself, even if he was no longer sure he knew *enough* demons. He certainly wasn't used to being the only human. "I'll find a better place to mingle. I wouldn't want to be mistaken for another round of refreshments."

The demon laughed, the sound rolling over itself like waves, and snapped a finger off the food, tapping their mouth with it. "Oh, son, I'm sure you'll find people who'll think that regardless."

"I'm sure I will," he said, mouth a little dry again. "Well, it'll make for an exciting party."

"It will, it will," the demon agreed. They narrowed those black eyes. Lacking sclera or iris, it was impossible to tell exactly where they were looking, but Renart felt the pressure of their gaze regardless. "I'm sure I could arrange some protection for a pretty boy like you. Would you like my company?"

"Thanks," Renart said, and smiled nicely. "But I'm waiting to meet someone."

"Is that so? More's the shame," the demon said, lips turning down in a slight frown. "You might regret it before the night's out. Do take care," they added coolly, and bit into the fingertip.

Renart left at a pace he hoped wouldn't be too obviously one of *escape*, more excited by the encounter than terrified by it. He managed to shoulder his way across to a part of the room far from the refreshment tables, tucked in between a potted plant and some hanging curtains.

Isolating himself still didn't mean he was left alone. Plenty of the partygoers had seen him, and he found himself fielding conversation after conversation, proposition after proposition, threat after threat. He kept the invitation clutched in his hand like a sweaty ward, a promise that he belonged here, was a guest. That he couldn't be harmed unless he permitted himself to be.

He *did* know demons well enough to know that, if at any point he let his guard down, said or did anything that might constitute permission... invitation or no invitation, he wouldn't have a chance.

"Excuse me," he murmured, dodging around a mass of limbs and eyes as it approached him, as if he had somewhere to be on the other side of the room.

Then, shortly, "No, thank you," he said politely, shifting behind a large ornamental vase to get out of the direct shadow of a tall man.

Repeatedly, he moved to new hiding places, avoided glances, ducked out of the way of approaching demons. He didn't think he'd ever watched his mouth so thoroughly, forced himself to be so affably neutral constantly, turned down so many offers and shrugged off so much intimidation. He'd never had the need to, and, more to the point, had never *wanted* to.

Finally, when he thought he might not be able to handle it any more, the prince arrived.

Hrahez looked almost exactly as Renart had seen him before—surprising, given that cubants were shapeshifters. If Renart could change form whenever he wanted, he didn't think he'd be the same way twice. But Hrahez was completely recognizable: long black hair, heavy curled horns lifting his chin high, draped robes. Perhaps it was one of the requirements of rank to be so easily known. A veil covered his face, which served to keep him distant from the others in some strange way.

The room fell silent when Hrahez entered. A hush spreading like the force of his presence had stolen their collective breath. It felt that way to Renart, at least, leaving his throat tight, his eyes wide. Hrahez was as beautiful as Renart had remembered. He thought that the demons surrounding him could probably hear how hard his heart was pounding. It almost felt like this had all been worth it even if he only just caught sight of him again.

No, he reminded himself. *It's not nearly enough.*

Glancing around the room, Hrahez's gaze fell on a petite demon—a beautiful creature, smooth all over as if carved from obsidian—and bowed with a smile, offering a hand. The obsidian demon took it, and the silence was abruptly broken as music sprang up from the orchestra pit.

Immediately, the room was awhirl with dancing. As Renart had suspected, everyone had only been waiting until Hrahez arrived before they could begin. Heart still hammering, Renart pressed himself back against the wall as demons split into pairs, trios, more, shapes gyrating and spinning throughout the room. He forced himself to breathe in deeply, ignoring the strange perfumes and unusual smells hanging in the air, and tried to calm down.

Hrahez was here. This was his chance—perhaps his *only* chance—but it was useless if Renart didn't find a way to approach him. He wasn't going to be the only one doing so, either. He was sure of that. Even if his motivations were different than theirs, plenty of the demons here would be trying to curry favor and get attention.

An introduction would be best, but there was no one to speak for him. He cast another gaze around the room in the hopes that the footman would reappear and Renart could convince him to help, but the demon was nowhere in sight. There was nobody else he even knew in passing, nobody who could introduce him.

In the moment of that realization, he felt himself grow calm. It was a weird type of focus, more adrenaline than actual peace, but it gave him room to think.

He had to do this entirely by himself.

Renart steeled himself, waiting for the ideal moment, watching the musicians and listening to the tune, trying to see how far along Hrahez's dance was. He ignored the dancers, other than to track Hrahez's position in the room. When it seemed like the song would end soon, he began pushing through the crowd. He didn't dare wait for the end, but starting too early was dangerous—there were plenty here who would run him over in their merriment, knock him to the ground, and crush him.

As if dancing himself, he dodged and wove through the spinning dancers. He was knocked back and forth with bruising strength whenever he misjudged and got clipped, but he refused to fall. He couldn't *afford* to fall. He kept an eye on the constantly-moving pair of Hrahez and the smooth-skinned demon, trying at all turns to angle himself towards them.

The music stopped. Frantic, Renart shoved

through the remaining few guests between himself and Hrahez, stepping forward just as Hrahez bowed and let go of the demon's hand. Renart's aggression caused a small commotion, hissed threats and muttered offense. It probably wasn't worse only because the prince's attention was now fixed his way.

He drew a breath and held a hand out. "May I have the next dance?" he asked, and heard his voice come out in a strained wheeze.

Horrified, he met the prince's eyes as best as he could through the distortion of his veil. Hrahez didn't seem startled, but the polite wall of his shaded expression shifted into something more genuine, corners of his eyes crinkling, amusement washing over his features. He laughed a moment later, ducking his head, then let the weight of his horns draw it back up and said, "So you're the human at my party."

"Y—"

"I'll dance with you," Hrahez agreed before Renart could even finish speaking, and took his hand.

The music started again, but Renart could hardly hear it over the rush of white noise in his head.

Tari'd had a noticeable aura of desire, but a soft one, a gentle one. The succubus in the village and the footman here were more so. Both had a strong appeal, a sense of restrained power that left arousal burning behind every brush of their fingers.

Touching Hrahez was like that, but taken to the extreme.

It wasn't as if it was different from his two recent encounters, not exactly. The feeling of their auras was nearly the same, but Hrahez's was *more*. If the others had seemed to have that power muted, in comparison, it rolled off Hrahez in waves. His hands touching Hrahez's made him ache to get closer, and when Hrahez pulled him in for the dance his breath hitched, body tight and flushed all over.

It felt like he was struck by lightning; the hair on his arms was standing up, nerves aching, and his skin over-sensitive. The scent of Hrahez surrounded Renart; he could smell him, taste him, *feel* him with every breath in. His mind reeled, almost in shock— hyper-focusing on small details, slow and laggy to process anything. It was like being underwater, like drowning. Desperate, he made himself look at the bottom of the veil Hrahez wore, watching the way it drifted as they moved, trying slowly to bring his wits back about himself again so he wouldn't waste his chance. But it was almost impossible, the air between them hazy and warm, this strong and familiar scent in his nostrils—

—and then Prince Hrahez stepped on his foot.

It *hurt*, and only the anklet he was wearing protected him at all from the sharp-edged hoof. As it was, the sudden weight and pressure jarred him out of his daze. He was still attracted, he was still *aroused*, but he wasn't lost in it.

"Sorry about that," Hrahez said cheerily. His voice wasn't at all apologetic, light but soft and smooth as honey, and he clipped Renart's foot again with his next step. "I'm not actually that good a dancer, but it's obligatory that I do a dance or two at this sort of thing."

Somehow, Renart managed to find his own voice. Shock faded into disbelief—was there anyone who'd believe that a demon prince, who'd lived for hundreds of years and was famous for his grand events, couldn't dance?

But then, Renart supposed, who would teach him if he didn't already know? He tried to keep that from his tone, as warmly neutral as he could manage. "Well, good thing I made the anklets, then. I wouldn't give up this chance for the world."

"Is that so? Good thing you don't have the world to give," Hrahez said with a grin and a quirked brow. He swept him around, hoof clipping Renart's shin. It stung, and Renart tried unsuccessfully to swallow a yelp, but Hrahez didn't seem to notice. "So you made these? It's just as well that you've got them. They're nicely made, too."

"I'm the local cobbler's son," Renart answered, voice a little strained. Then, daringly, "If you want new footwear, I could make you a pair of anything you like."

"Do you think you could? I haven't found many nice shoes for hooves."

Renart grinned up at him. "I'm inventive," he said, and wiggled a foot on his next step. "Just look at *these*. I can't wear anything on the bottom of my feet, but I'm pretty proud of my ability to work with what I've got."

"It *is* pretty clever," Hrahez admitted. "So your bare soles are unprotected?"

The conversation was so simple, so easy, that Renart felt his spirits lifting. The pain of Hrahez's wayward hooves aside, it was like walking on air.

He was finally here. Not just held close, not just dancing, but talking with Hrahez like one normal person to another. As if they weren't demon and human, prince and cobbler. Getting to do so, he found that Hrahez wasn't just interesting.

Renart *liked* him.

It was partially Hrahez's natural charisma,

certainly, but there was a familiar comfort to him, an easy-going tone to the way he talked, affably affectionate, that made him want to respond in kind.

He swallowed and made himself find the conversation again. Soles. Right. "That's the agreement I made, so that's how it is." He shrugged a little against Hrahez's grip, trying to seem nonchalant, and managed not to flinch as a hoof pinched the unprotected edge of his foot to the floor. "I already pushed my luck far enough twisting this verbal agreement from one kind of 'soul' to another—I wasn't going to try to break my word to a demon on top of that!"

"Wise of you," Hrahez said with amusement. "In fact—"

The music came to a stop.

Hrahez stopped dancing along with it and fell silent, still holding Renart close to him. Renart's stomach suddenly clenched, knowing that there were only seconds now before Hrahez would pull away, find another partner. It was too fast, he thought desperately. Too soon. He came all this way and it was wonderful, sure, but it couldn't be over yet...!

As he scrambled to find something to say, something to do, something that could keep this from ending, Hrahez leaned down, veiled lips brushing against his jaw.

"In exactly an hour," Hrahez breathed into his ear, veil gusting against his cheek, "leave the party and come to my room." He murmured directions, and Renart forced himself to focus on them and not how hard he'd gotten at the closeness of Hrahez's body, at the murmur directly against him. Out the door Hrahez had entered by, down the hall, the third door to the left, down another hall, take a right, up a stairway, a hall to a door at the end, another stairway, a hall to another door.

He shuddered roughly, licking his lips. "Yes," he breathed back.

And at that, Hrahez dropped his hand and pulled away, leaving him almost staggering. The prince whirled back into the party with good cheer and apparent lack of interest in Renart himself.

It suited Renart perfectly. He stumbled across the room, leaning against a wall near the door out, and watched the clock. It separated him somewhat from the throng of demons clamoring for Hrahez's attention, though he noticed that he was getting no small amount of glowering and irritated looks.

No wonder, he thought. Hrahez had spent a few precious minutes on him and not on any of them.

~~*

A little over fifty minutes after the whispered message, Hrahez announced that he was retiring, and told the rest of the gathered throng to enjoy the party for him. He breezed past Renart without even a look as he headed out the door. Renart didn't let it discourage him. He knew what he'd been invited to. Out. Down the hall. Third door, left. Hall. Right. Up, hall, up, door—

Soon.

He tried not to be too overt about it, tried not to give himself completely away, tried not to stare at the clock. But with less than ten minutes left, he didn't feel like he could risk losing any time. Even as the demons gathered around him again, he just shook his head. It didn't matter anymore if they were inviting or threatening him. Either way, he played dumb. Acted like he was star-struck, overcome by being held by an incubus of that much power. It seemed to work.

He couldn't leave at one hour on the dot, since he had to wait until it seemed nobody was looking. Those few minutes past his deadline were agonizing, but finally he slipped away and darted out the door Hrahez had left through.

The feel of the manor was immediately different. While the main hall of the mansion was lavish and opulent, it was immediately clear to him that the rest hadn't been cared for in the slightest since its abandonment. The back halls were dusty and dark, with broken tile and cobwebs filling them. If the echoing music weren't floating down the hallway behind him, he would have started to imagine himself totally alone. Renart found himself wondering if even that main room and the gardens he'd seen had *truly* been so luxurious, or if there had been some kind of magic involved.

Still, even if he suddenly felt a little like he was trespassing, it wasn't like that was off-putting. If anything, it was exciting—under normal circumstances, he'd never be able to be here, but he'd managed to not only come but do so *legitimately*. Was invited not just to the party but to Hrahez's bedroom. Out of all the people in that room, Hrahez had picked *him* to spend time with.

Renart took a deep breath, and forced himself to focus on the path in front of him, winding around as he followed the directions to the first stairway. If he worked himself up to the point he forgot where to go, he wouldn't be ending up in *anyone's* bedroom.

He took the stairs two at a time, half out of eagerness and half because they didn't seem entirely stable—the wood rotted, the carpet moth-eaten. Going up them quickly got it over with faster, though despite his initial concerns, they didn't seem about ready to give away. The wood shifted uneasily under his feet, but didn't feel *mushy* or anything too dangerous.

The hallway at the next landing was another story. He brought himself up short, drawing a sharp breath in.

It had once been lined with glass-covered paintings and mirrors; some devastation had occurred here, and most had fallen. Some, still on the walls, were simply smashed. A chandelier, too, had fallen in the middle of the hallway, and while the candles on it were unlit and there was no risk of fire, the whole situation had left the entire hall covered in glass.

His stomach clenched, then sank, and then he *sighed*. Of course, he thought, demons weren't known for making things easy, and Hrahez was infamous for playing games, for testing people. And Hrahez *had* shown great interest in his uncovered feet.

"So this is how it is," he said aloud, and shuffled a foot forward cautiously.

His feet had toughened a little during his time without shoes, but not *that* much, and he knew it. All he could do was brace himself for the pain and do his best to nudge aside the glass with the sides of his feet. As he moved forward, he did so at a snail's pace, shuffling each foot as lightly as he could to clear a small swept path before cautiously putting his weight down on it.

Even so, he cut them. They split and bled, cut into

by small glass fragments he wasn't able to move aside. The pain was a dull, throbbing mess that made him clench his jaw and his fists to keep from crying out. The rush of adrenaline that came with the pain made it hard to move at an even pace—his mind kept telling him that if he ran it'd be over with faster, just like on the stairs, and he had to force himself to pick his way across slowly regardless.

He lost track of time, completely absorbed in the task. He wasn't able to pay attention to anything beyond his deliberate, careful sweeping motions, doing his best to ignore the pain. The throb of agony felt like an inverted image of the shocks of arousal he'd felt when they were dancing. This was a test of his stubbornness, he was sure of that.

But that was one thing he'd never been lacking in.

When he realized there was no more glass in front of him he stood dumbly for a few moments, as if waiting for the trap, then crumpled forward with a groan. He must have spent hours, he thought, though maybe that was just how it had *felt*. Even so, he let himself lose some more time by sitting on the desiccated carpet, gently squeezing glass splinters out of his feet, watching his blood drip down. He couldn't even bind his feet, he thought sadly. It wasn't even the lack of anything to bind with—he'd cut up his vest if he thought it would work. But he'd tried before back when his feet were newly bare, and the bandages wouldn't stay on. His curse affected them as well.

Well, that was just how things were, he thought firmly. He was through now, and one hallway closer to the prince. Besides, what could he do—turn around to leave and walk back through the glass? *No thank you.* He wasn't giving up now, not when he was this close.

Renart got to his feet again, brushed his hands carefully off on his trousers, and continued along the path with as jaunty a step as he could manage, trailing bloody footprints behind himself until he reached the end of the hall, with a door at the end and one to either side.

He paused.

Suddenly, he was no longer so sure that he remembered the path. *It was through the door at the end, not the right again?* Then a stairway. It was up two floors total—wasn't it? The pain had distracted him.

But he didn't have time to hesitate.

He took the door at the end, took the stairs on the other side up, and was weirdly relieved when he opened the door at the top onto a hallway liberally covered in salt.

"Really?" he asked aloud, laughing. "Is this necessary?"

At least it proved he was on the right path.

There was no way to keep the salt from his cuts, and he didn't try, just shrugged and strode forward, still laughing softly to himself. That took him no time at all, and when he reached the door at the end, his feet were stinging and aflame, his entire body aching with both anticipation and agony. He could hardly tell which was which anymore.

He stood in the salt at the end of the hall and knocked on the door. It opened after the second knock, the still-veiled prince glancing him over. Behind the cloth, his features seemed almost surprised.

"Even with bare soles you did it," he said, tone taken aback. "Are you an overeager fool?"

"I am," Renart said, a little giddy.

Hrahez shook his head and drew him inside with one hand. With the other, he pushed the veil up, revealing his warm green eyes that seemed to hold glittering stars inside them, a strong nose, curved lips. Renart's heart leaped in a triumphant sense of realization, and he leaned up to kiss Hrahez.

He was, in that moment, completely confident that Hrahez wouldn't reject him.

There wasn't even a moment of delay. Hrahez's mouth curved against his in a smile, and Renart was pulled into the kiss. It was firm and warm and absolutely radiated genuine affection.

Renart had a moment to think, *I thought so,* before he melted into it, kneading his fingers where they pressed against Hrahez's shoulders.

The kiss deepened, a pointed tongue winding its way into his mouth, too long and too agile. He met it with his own, letting Hrahez explore, finally managing to loosen his grip enough to allow his hands to start to wander. They moved over Hrahez's chest, down his sides, hungrily touching.

Hrahez stepped back toward the bed, pulling Renart with him. Renart advanced eagerly—and then put his weight down on a cut section of his foot, hissing with pain into the kiss.

Abruptly, Hrahez pulled back, twisting and scooping Renart up to carry him. "Little fool," he said, his tone not unkind, "I can't believe you really did it."

"Of course you can," Renart managed, as Hrahez brought him the few steps over to the bed and put him down on it with only a little jolt. "You're the one who set this all up."

"Walking across glass to get fucked is a little unnecessary." Hrahez knelt beside the bed, taking hold of one of Renart's feet behind the heel and lifting it to take a look. "But you're the one who's willing to do such undesirable things." He didn't sound scornful, despite his words. He sounded *eager*, Renart thought.

Renart let out a breath as Hrahez found a shard of glass in there he'd missed and squeezed it free. "If you don't want me to do it, don't put glass on the floor. You just wanted to know I'd do it for you."

"Yes, I *did*, but—"

"Are you lonely?" Renart murmured. "I'm sure plenty of people want you, but you don't go looking for them. You're the prince, after all. Our eyes met, you know, at one of your parades. I can't be the only one who was looking just at you... no, the whole crowd was. There was no reason for you to meet my eyes in particular. You certainly wouldn't seek me out, I'd thought, so I'd look for you instead. Oh, you made me feel..."

How to describe it? That moment of hunger, the desire to challenge him like he'd challenged the whole world as a child. *Snap me up. Devour me. I dare you.*

Hrahez's eyes flicked up to his again and held his gaze for a moment, hard to read. Then, without responding otherwise, he lifted Renart's foot higher, kissing the arch.

There was a rush of warmth and Renart shuddered as arousal hit him. Even through that feeling, he could feel another strange sensation, a tightness on his foot, a tingling, a relief from how much it hurt—*It's healing*, he thought, a bit surprised. *He's healing me.*

Lowering his foot to the bed, Hrahez picked up the other and did it again: checked it over for any remaining glass, kissed it, healed it. Renart supported himself on his elbows, watching that heavy-horned head bowed over his foot, and tried to breathe evenly. Part of the effect was just Hrahez's nature as an incubus, the arousing aura that his entire breed had. But the rest...

The rest, he thought a little hazily, was just the moment. Finally being here with Hrahez after all his planning, all his efforts. Keeping him company. Talking to him so comfortably.

The healing came in a rush, the cessation of pain so complete that the space it left behind could only be filled with his desperate desire.

This foot, Hrahez didn't lower—he kept it raised, mouth slowly kissing across the sole, lips lingering on the toes. Renart drew a slow, sharp breath at the deliberate intention in that motion, shuddered as Hrahez's mouth closed around his big toe, tongue winding between them. *Must taste bad*, he thought briefly, and choked on a sound that was as much laugh as moan.

"Hm?" Hrahez murmured, and he could feel that against his foot, the warm rush of air, the vibration of his mouth.

I can meet that invitation halfway, he thought. He shifted, running his other foot down Hrahez's stomach, resting it just over his groin. "The salt," he said, in explanation.

Hrahez snorted inelegantly, and his long tongue slid down over the sole of Renart's foot like he meant to lick the salt right up. Hrahez clearly didn't care, eager and heated. Hrahez might not have cared, Renart thought dazedly, even if there had been any glass left.

Renart shifted against the bed, grinding his other foot down on Hrahez's groin, trying to nudge his robes aside. He didn't feel like he was getting anywhere with that, but didn't much mind. One way or another, he could feel his foot rolling against the hard length of Hrahez's cock, feel himself pushing and pressing against it—it felt good, *amazing*, knowing that he was turning Hrahez on in return.

Hrahez exhaled softly as his tongue pulled at Renart's toes. Hrahez's hands were busy unbuckling the anklet on the foot he was holding, but once he'd finished with that, he let go almost at once and pulled his robes up and apart around his waist, letting Renart touch him directly.

That made Renart's heart beat faster—not just the shifting, firm warmth under his foot, but the idea that Hrahez was this hungry for his touch as well. Renart rubbed his foot up against Hrahez's cock, pushing it up to his stomach, toes catching and pulling at the head. The angle wasn't the best, but it gave him room to grind his heel in at the base just above Hrahez's balls.

He was going to check in, ask if it was good, but his eyes met Hrahez's again and he found he didn't need to. Those green eyes were heated, so intense they'd turned almost gold, with the sideways pupils flared wide. His mouth was hot against Renart's other foot, sucking and pulling at his toes, tongue sliding down across the near-ticklish underside of his foot to wrap around his ankle and back up. Renart shuddered helplessly at the sight, hips rocking up against nothing, skin feeling almost too-tight with his need. He was overheated, overwhelmed in his good clothes and tight breeches.

But he didn't try to ask for more, not yet, and didn't try to touch himself. He *wanted* to, but there was something too good about the moment to want to interrupt, about Hrahez playing with one foot, his other foot toying with Hrahez. He ground his foot hard for a moment, almost roughly, and then shifted to push Hrahez's cock back down to his thigh, dragging his sole along it from heel to toes.

Hrahez moaned.

The sound rocked through Renart as if it had physical force, stroking along every nerve in his body like fingers raking through hair. He shuddered, arching a bit, his one foot slipping in Hrahez's grasp, his other grinding roughly against his cock.

Hrahez seemed, for a moment, like he wasn't going to act—then shifted abruptly, wrapping his free hand around Renart's foot on his cock and began thrusting, rocking up against it, jerking himself off against the sole. Renart's thighs ached from his attempt to find balance with his other foot still lifted high in the air, but before he could do anything but open his mouth to ask for help, Hrahez was already letting go and letting it slide back to the bed.

Hrahez looked up at Renart while rocking against him, grinned, and came against his foot.

It was fast, Renart thought through his half-dazed confusion. The waves of Hrahez's pleasure were a tangible presence in the room that made breathing difficult. *Deliberately fast*, he thought a moment later, as if Hrahez, being an incubus, had just chosen release to calm himself down and draw the whole experience out. That was the look in the demon's eyes, anyway, a heavy determination.

"My Lord—"

"Enough of that," Hrahez murmured. "You came here to find me, didn't you? Use my name."

"*Hrahez*," Renart croaked, shuddering. He was too

turned on. He almost couldn't think, almost envied the demon's ability to regain control like that. If *he* just let himself come now—and it was a tempting thought, even untouched—he'd just be tired, he thought.

Though with Hrahez in front of him, real, able to be touched, maybe not too tired to go on.

Hrahez barely gave him a moment to think regardless, slowly lowering Renart's foot to the bed. Thick come stuck to his sole, sliding down; Hrahez didn't bother to clean him off at all, just let him drip onto the sheets and went for his breeches.

Renart groaned again, reaching for him, finding the heavy curve of Hrahez's horns. As he grasped them and curled his fingers around them as best he could, Hrahez's eyes flicked up to meet him again, as though he were actually asking permission.

The softness in his eyes, the consideration in the gesture after the pain and the salt and all the rest, was almost overwhelming. He couldn't remember having been with a demon who had asked a second time once they were already into the thick of things. Renart nodded, helpless. "Yes," he said.

Hrahez smiled briefly, then swallowed him down with no hesitation, Renart's cock sliding deep into his throat, long winding tongue wrapping around the base. It was blindingly hot, tight, and he felt pinned by Hrahez's gaze. He couldn't look away, entranced, rocking into Hrahez's mouth as he pulled and sucked and wound his tongue against him all at once.

It was too much.

"I won't last," he croakedt. "I'm sorry, but—"

With a laugh, Hrahez pulled back, pointed tongue stroking through the slit. "I'll keep you going," he promised, his tone low and warm. Although Renart knew he should probably read some threat into it—he knew *demons*—he didn't feel a sense of danger at all.

"All right," Renart managed thickly, more than a little distracted, and let Hrahez swallow him down again.

He came twice like that. The first time was soon after his words, hands white-knuckled with tension on Hrahez's horns. The second time was slow, Hrahez's mouth working him into hardness again, taking his time with him. Hrahez teased him for such an agonizingly long time that he couldn't handle it any more, came almost more for relief than pleasure, sobbing out and gripping tightly to his horns.

After, Renart barely had a chance to catch his breath before Hrahez surged up, shoving him down into the bed. He leaned over Renart, forcing arousal back into his body again with a surge of demonic energy.

It was more than Renart could handle, and everything he wanted. He'd only dreamed of this, to be overcome completely and brought back over and over again. He let out an involuntary sob, arching. It was amazing and painful, perfect torture. He felt wrecked, brain in tatters, completely unable to do more than grasp onto the form over him, holding tight, *feeling* him.

He would have accepted anything, taken anything, but Hrahez seemed to realize he was falling apart and was almost gentle, rutting against him with their cocks held tight together in one hand. Hrahez braced himself on one elbow, hair falling around them, and worked them in a steady, quick pace, murmuring to him.

It took a moment for him to make out words through the exhausted shocks of pleasure. They were praises—soft, light praises. He writhed at the sound as he was pulled closer to orgasm again with every pass of Hrahez's hand, with the sensation of his cock squeezed against Hrahez's. Hrahez kept complimenting him in soft murmurs: *good, sweet, lovely*. All the while seeming as eager as Renart felt, holding him and rolling against him.

Renart pushed himself up, grinding frantically, moving over and over again, and tried to give as good as he got. Tried to make Hrahez feel as good as he did.

He groaned as he came again, shuddering hard through the force of it. Hrahez let out a moan at the sudden slickness in his hand, and followed a moment later, head dropping forward heavily, semen spattering up across Renart's stomach. The pleasure tore through Renart, leaving him feeling raw and shaken and sated. Tired and warm, pushed supernaturally beyond his body's limits, but not *drained*. Not like he usually was with cubants. If Hrahez had been drinking from him at all, it had been subtly only, tasting and not taking energy any faster than could be restored.

Even though he could barely focus, that drove the last nail into the metaphorical coffin. Renart's suspicions might not be *confirmed*, but they were awfully, delightfully plausible.

They lay there gasping for a long few moments. Renart shivered through the aftershocks of pleasure, indulging in the long moment of listening to Hrahez's breath slowly get back under his control.

"Mm. We done?" Renart asked finally, his tongue heavy and disobedient. His limbs were even weightier, and he'd sunk back against the bed in an enormous sprawl. The wetness on his feet had cooled in the air and he was starting to feel chilly as the pleasure ebbed, but he couldn't bring himself to move. To his delighted surprise, Hrahez tucked himself warmly against Renart's side, curled against him so closely that he started to suspect they were actually cuddling.

Hrahez laughed. "Oh, now, I don't know," he said. "If I were done with you, I'd feel obliged to throw you out."

"Hmm." Now was the time to say it, if ever. Renart tried to shake his brain back into some semblance of order. "Well," he said, sitting up and running his fingers through his hair, catching immediately on snags, "'f you're gonna throw m'out, c'n I..." He worked his mouth, tried to enunciate more clearly. "Can I have one last look at my soles first?" Then, with exhausted humor, "I didn't get to say a proper goodbye, and you people know the importance of a man's sole."

Beside him, Hrahez had gone very still. Renart stole a glance, finding Hrahez's eyes wide and surprised, his mouth open. The overall expression on his face was strangely vulnerable as a result.

Renart found he really, *really* liked that.

"What...?" Hrahez asked finally, his voice extremely tentative.

Despite his certainty, Renart's stomach clenched a little. He could be wrong. If he were, this would be a terrible insult. But he thought he'd realized, and he needed to know for sure. Needed Hrahez to know *he* knew. "Well, you're the demoness who took them?" Then, even less certain but not willing to second-guess himself, "I think you're the footman as well. The one who lavished such attention on my feet before I got into the ball."

For a moment, no reaction showed on Hrahez's

face. He stared at Renart with that strange, open, curious expression, like Renart were suddenly speaking in tongues. Slowly, horribly, Renart's heart dropped.

And then Hrahez let out a breath, starting to laugh giddily. "How did you know?"

The rush of relief hit Renart so hard that he was abruptly grateful he was already sitting down. "Your eyes." Renart tapped his own cheekbone, then felt a little silly about it. "Our eyes met when you were riding that one day and I don't think I'd ever forget how they looked. You changed everything else completely but your eyes were the same all three times." That deep, gold-flecked green. He watched Hrahez's horizontally-slitted pupils contract, then dilate again slowly as he reacted to what he was hearing.

He licked his lips shakily, and went on before Hrahez could answer him. "I didn't know until I saw your eyes without the veil. I think—I don't understand why, but—I think, you were as interested in me as I was in you, back during that parade."

Hrahez laughed again, the sound sudden and light-hearted. He flopped across the bed, reaching down to rummage underneath it. The long line of his back trailing into his tail seemed relaxed; Renart wanted to reach out and run his fingers along it, but resisted for now. Everything felt too uncertain.

"Awfully smelly things," Hrahez said, coming up with a small box and opening it. He plucked one of Renart's old shoe soles out with his fingertips. "But a bit of a trophy, regardless. I admit they charm me."

"Like I do?" Renart asked, and let himself indulge a little, running his fingers along Hrahez's side. "I can't believe you came to me three times. Why?"

Hrahez snorted and dropped them back into the box. "Yes, you incorrigible thing, just like you charm me." He turned his face away a little as he put the box down on the bed between them, slowly and with care.

"It was just interest," Hrahez said after a moment, sounding almost hesitant. "I wouldn't read too much into it, if I were you. The entire crowd was hungry, passively wanting me, but you wanted me in a different way. A discordant note in all that mess. I thought for a moment you might shove your way through the crowd and throw yourself under my horse. To my ability to sense desire, it was like you were screaming, 'Come and get me'. It made it difficult to forget about you. I kept wanting to know more. So, yes, I walked past your door deliberately that day."

Was that actually a spot of color on Hrahez's cheeks?

Renart beamed, holding his arms open. His heart *sang*. All this time, all these months, all that agonizing about how to go to him, and Hrahez had been doing the same. Triumph and genuine happiness mingled together so fully that they became a feeling he couldn't begin to describe, tears in his eyes, relief shaking him.

"Come here, then," Renart said. "You aren't ever throwing me out, are you?" No focus, his mum had said. Always faffing about. Chasing his dreams. *And why*, he thought, *was that ever a sign I couldn't focus?*

He'd just needed to find what he wanted to focus on.

Hrahez sighed. "I suppose I'm not," he said, a sullen fondness on his face. He pushed the box aside, dragged Renart down, and pulled the blankets up over them both.

Pulled them up too far, Renart realized. Probably didn't even notice it with his hooves.

"My feet are out," he said.

Hrahez propped himself up on an elbow. "And?"

Renart gave him a wide-eyed look. Tried to say it with his face: *Shouldn't you know already?* "They're cold. Since they belong to you, treat them nicely."

Hrahez snorted. "Like you can complain about that after everything you've done to them," he said.

But he leaned down and tucked Renart in anyway.

BEHIND
bars

Chapter One

The last thing Pelerin Stone wanted to do the evening after arguing with his son was *work*. He'd have to be ready with smiles and easy chatter that he just wasn't feeling. But it needed to be done whether or not he wanted to. It was important, and bigger than either of them.

Strained and tired, Pel got ready for the day: polishing wine glasses, wiping down the bar, and hefting casks up the steep steps from the cellar. The cooks were working slowly today, which only made his mood worse. He tried not to show it, because they didn't exactly deserve it—not when his real problem lay elsewhere—and because they'd almost certainly work slower just to spite him if he snapped at them.

The inn opened early in the evening and had just unlocked its doors, which meant Pel was behind. Customers didn't stop for bad days, and it wouldn't be long before people started rolling in. He imagined he'd be seeing the Villem boys soon; they were almost always the first to arrive, and they had big appetites. Normally, he'd consider that a good thing.

And they'd be the first of many. The inn was a popular place, which was good when he was in a fine mood and everyone was getting their work done but less good right now, when he really just wanted to have a break. But Dolana was not a town with a lot of places to relax. The places the Inquisition had vetted as safe and free from demonic influence were, as a result, in demand.

The bell over the door jingled, and Pel looked up with an automatic smile that he hoped wouldn't seem forced. Was the stew ready yet? The Villem boys would want—

—It wasn't the Villem boys. To his even greater surprise, it wasn't anybody he knew at all.

The stranger was a tall and lean woman, probably in her late thirties. She had no chest to speak of, but her hips were wide and her facial features delicate. Under her heavily brocaded vest, she wore a fine shirt stained with sweat and dust from the road. She'd likely been riding to get here, judging from the style of breeches and high boots she was wearing. A heavy-seeming sack was slung over her shoulder.

Pel kept himself from frowning out of sheer force of will. Visitors to Dolana were rare. He let rooms, of course, but most of his patrons were citizens who needed a brief place to stay—youths moving out who hadn't found a place to lease, folks rebuilding after a fire, people like that. He hadn't had cause to actually rent them out to a traveler for over a year now. Anyone coming from out of the city had to pass the gate inspection, and even the innocent ones tended to steer clear of that much hassle and keep on the main road toward the next town instead.

Still, she looked human enough. Her skin was a warm shade of light brown with a smattering of freckles, and even if her eyes were a startlingly light blue, they were well within the normal human range.

She caught his gaze and gave him a once-over in return, blatant about it and favoring him with a smile. He straightened, surprised by how forthright she was—but then, he kept himself dressed and groomed to have a good effect on patrons. He was dressed in a clean, cream-colored shirt that he left open at the neck and rolled up at the elbows to keep himself casual, and it was perfectly fitted to his frame. His brown hair might have gone sandy as the years caught up to him, but he kept it short-trimmed and neat, and he kept himself free from facial hair. The hairless lines where his scars were made him look a bit threatening once he went to stubble.

She headed for the bar, and her bag hit the floor with a satisfying thump as she slid onto a stool across from him, grinning. "Goodness, but am *I* glad to see this place." Her gaze immediately slid to the scar on his cheek, lingering on the three faded claw marks. He kept himself from raising a hand to them out of long practice only.

Her voice had the soft husk of a smoker. He glanced her over again for other signs of that—wrinkles at the corners of the mouth or the yellowing around the fingernails—but came up with nothing.

Pel looked up again, widening his smile a little. He knew it gave him dimples that worked well with the broad set of his jaw, and they distracted people from the scars. "A traveler?" he asked. "We don't see many of your type around here. Welcome to Dolana."

"I imagine not, judging from the interrogation I got at the gate." The woman tossed her loose black curls back off her shoulder. She'd either not bound her hair for travel or had taken it down before entering, so he surmised that she, too, liked to make an impression. "Do you have rooms to rent? Or a meal—I'm starving." She winked at him, playful.

"We have both." Smiling affably, he pretended he

hadn't seen the hints of interest behind the wink. He might be happy to use his looks to get money and information when he needed them, but he wasn't looking to lead her on beyond that. "I'll get the cooks to bring you out a bowl of stew." Gods willing they'd actually finished making it. "Rooms are forty a night and include dinner. Can I get you a drink to help wash down the dust—"

Of the road, he'd meant to say, but as Pel had turned to indicate the stairwell up to the rooms, his son, Bruant, appeared in the stairwell, slouching. Pel had kept Bruant's wavy brown hair short for him when he was young, but recently Bruant had wanted to grow it out, and now it seemed to go everywhere *except* where it was supposed to be.

He was dressed to go out with friends, flat cap pushing his hair down in a way that only made its fall worse. The wool vest he was wearing was one he'd purchased during the winter, eager to wear it when spring came around, but he'd had the last bit of growth spurt before that could happen. It stuck to his body so tightly it could have been fixed there. Pel saw the buttons strain as he and Bruant made eye contact and Bruant sucked a breath in.

Pel counted his blessings that whatever new scene was to happen between them today wouldn't happen *yet*. Not with a visitor here.

It had been wishful thinking. Bruant came over, hands shoved into his pockets—still radiating tension and anger from that morning, his black eyes a little wild and his jaw clenched enough to stick out.

"Dad." Bruant leaned on the bar right next to the stranger, not paying her a moment's attention, his hands clenched into fists. "We need to talk."

Pel felt a muscle in his jaw jump as he tried to maintain his friendly smile. "I thought we talked enough earlier, Bru," he said, as lightly as he could manage.

"I'm nowhere near done with you." Bruant was clearly trying for threatening but not quite making it. His fine features, so like his mother's, were tight and drawn. "Ditch work for a bit."

"Family problems?" the traveler asked, both her brows raised. "I don't mean to interrupt, but I'm hoping to at least get a room settled and some food and drink in front of me before you two have whatever argument you've got in mind."

"I'm so sorry," Pel told her. Bruant had been moody ever since he'd hit puberty, but their argument seemed to have set him off worse than ever. He turned back to Bruant. "Not now. We'll talk later."

"But—"

"*Later*," Pel said, letting his smile fall finally. *Take the damn hint, Bru.*

For a moment, he wasn't sure Bruant would go along with it. But, eyes going darker and sulkier, Bruant turned away with a jerky motion. "Fine." He glanced aside at the stranger, his expression hidden from Pel. "You could find a better place to stay than *this* hole," he said, then turned, heading out. His mood was almost visible, like he could be trailing a black cloud behind him.

Pel watched him leave, then quickly turned back to the stranger and forced the smile back onto his face, though it felt awkward now. "I'm so sorry," he repeated. "He's at a difficult age."

"Around twenty, I'd wager," the stranger said, looking more amused than offended as she gazed after Bruant. "I could find a better place to stay, huh? He sure seems angry at you for something."

Pel sighed. "He misses his mother and I'm a poor substitute as a parent," he said. "You have any kids?"

"I don't think so," the woman said with a dismissive laugh. Clearly not a fan of children. She held out her hand. "I'm Tari."

Only a first name, and an unusual one at that. He blinked but took her hand, and matched her firm grip as they shook. "I'm sorry, is that a nickname? I'm going to have to ask your full name if you want a room. We do keep records."

"Not a problem," she assured him, flashing him what was clearly meant to be a winning smile. "Toutarelle Walker. About that stew? And an ale, if you have one. Is that why he was saying I shouldn't stay here—no beer?"

A local name after all. She might have come from a nearby fiefdom.

Although anyone could fake a name.

"I assure you we have beer. I'll get that for you."

It only took Pel a few moments to get both from the back, and he returned carrying a bowl and a pint. During that time, she had shifted around on her seat and was watching the crowd of regulars with an air of assessment, though she turned back to him as he approached and smiled as he put her meal down on the bar.

"A welcome sight." She picked out coins from a bag she kept inside her vest and tossed them on the counter. The pile was enough for the night, and several more pints as well. "I'm *starving*. Oh, and I'm not sure how many days I'll be staying. My horse developed a limp and I need to resupply while I'm in town. Is that going to be a problem?"

Likely more of a problem for you than for me, he thought. "Not so long as you've got more where that came from," he said instead, sweeping the coin behind the bar. "How long did the guard keep you?"

"About six hours," Tari said, and groaned dramatically. "I made it to town about noon and was looking forward to a civilized meal, but once I said I wanted entry, they dragged me off and questioned me about my business for *ages*. I guess they finally realized I wasn't anything to be suspicious of, but I won't lie that it shook me up a little."

She didn't look shaken up, though. She grinned at him as if her story was actually just some kind of footnote to an adventure. Then again, it might be. Demons hunted pretty freely outside the towns. If you weren't one of them, you didn't travel alone without a good way to defend yourself, and certainly not unless you were willing to face the risk.

"So what *is* your business?"

"I trade in jewels," she said easily, gesturing below the counter—probably toward her bag. "Go to the cities that have the good mines, barter and bargain, get raw gems. Then I trek back to the places where they're harder to come by, polish and cut and get them primed for sale. I usually go north to Gabion to stock up, but after the mine closure I decided to take my chances going out east to Levisham."

Levisham? That's a demon-controlled fiefdom. He felt the familiar chill in his hands, an awareness of hearing something suspicious, something that the Inquisition might want to know.

But so far it still fit her story. Levisham was a mining city. The gate guards would have asked about that sort of thing as well. It probably wasn't the type of information the Inquisition would be looking for.

"Sounds like dangerous work," he said. "Where are you from?"

"Most recently, Potfeld."

He was pretty sure Potfeld was a demonic fiefdom, but he couldn't recall if it was one without human slavery. In the end, it didn't matter, though. *Whether their dark lords like to crush or pamper them, humans are still exposed to them like a child to the plague.*

"I've heard that's a nice place," he said affably. "But Levisham's a good distance away. I'm surprised you're traveling alone."

"Well, that's why I need to resupply." Tari spread her arms wide as if to encompass the entire town within her potential supplies. "I do all right, but being able to barter when I need to or fight when I must, that's the key to travel, isn't it?"

He laughed, leaning on the bar. "Fair enough," he said. "No husband to bring with you?"

Tari's eyes widened briefly. Then she laughed too, the sound a little rough. "A previous relationship of mine recently ended," she said, without any trace of regret. "I suppose I'm in the market. Why, you volunteering to accompany me?" She winked.

"Oh, you couldn't pay me to leave." Pel kept his voice light. "I've got my home here."

"Shame," she said with a wink. "I might consider accepting your companionship. At least, if you smile at me with those dimples again."

He didn't mean to, but a laugh slipped out of him at how forthright that was.

"Oh, yes, that's what I like." Her eyes seemed to brighten as she grinned at him with a flash of white teeth.

"You," he began, but was interrupted as the Villem brothers rolled in at last, arm in arm and laughing uproariously, calling for beer. It was poor timing; she was opening up more, and he was sure he could have gotten more information out of her.

But he could hardly ignore the other patrons. Pel turned away to do his regular job rather than the one he did on the side.

~~*

The bar became too busy for him to dwell on Tari. And it got rowdy fast, with the usuals seeming almost riled up by the presence of an outsider. He did his best to at least keep an eye on her as he chatted up others and handed out drinks—made easier by how she'd made herself the center of attention, flirting with just about anyone who'd give her the time of day.

It embarrassed him to watch. Certainly, it wasn't something he was used to. The few women who came to the bar to flirt tended to pick tables to themselves where they could chat people up properly, not plunk themselves down right in front of him at the bar, and were easier to ignore. It was a relief when she stopped downing drinks and leaned over the counter to get the key to her room from him.

"Can I show you upstairs?" he asked, holding the key out. "They won't break anything in the five minutes I'll step away—"

The younger Villem brother, Loir, snatched the key before she could get it. He, along with his brother Furt, had been competing for her attention all evening. "I'll take care of that for you, Stone."

"Charming," Tari told Loir, smirking and slinging an arm around his waist. To Pel she said, "Don't worry, sir. It seems this gentleman knows the way."

Pel watched as the two of them headed up the stairs, arm in arm. They'd almost vanished from sight when Furt slammed a hand down on the bar, yanking Pel's attention back. "Another drink," Furt snarled, visibly sulking.

Slightly taken aback, Pel poured a drink and leaned forward. As Furt vented out his annoyance that the younger, smaller brother had pulled her when Furt had failed, Pel just nodding understandingly, paying little attention. The two of them were always incorrigible, and Pel had listened to the same refrain from both of them often enough.

Tari didn't come down again, and at one in the morning, when Pel shooed out the last of the stragglers and began to clean, he could only assume that Loir would be staying the night with her.

Bruant, too, hadn't returned, even though he should have been home hours earlier. Pel tried to tamp down his irritation. The cooks might clean their stations—except when they thought they could get away with a shoddy job—but the rest of the bar was left for him and Bruant to clean, and it wasn't a one-person job.

Well, if Bruant was spending the night out, Pel would just have to do the majority of it in the morning. Tonight would just be for sopping up whatever was likely to be harder to clean when dry.

It was a half hour later, with the worst of the spills mopped, when the sound of the key in the door let him know that Bruant was home. He came in with a gust of cold evening air, looking more tired than angry now, his jacket closed and one arm inside it.

The exhaustion on his face seemed to burn off when he saw Pel. "Dad," he said, voice strained. His entire body almost vibrated with a sudden tension.

"Son," Pel shot back, in the same irritable tone Bruant had used on him. "You're late."

"I got held up." Bruant seemed to chew on the inside of his mouth, an anxious gesture more than an angry one. "About that stranger…"

"What about her?"

"Are you going to turn her in?" he asked sharply. "From what you said, sounds like you're in so good with *them* that if you're suspicious, she's gone."

Pel sighed. "No. Not if there's no reason to," he said. "Keep your damn voice down. She's staying the night, you know. Probably several, maybe longer."

Bruant's chin jerked up. "You aren't even denying that you would," he said, shocked.

The gesture left a pang in Pel's chest, hauntingly familiar. For a long moment, Pel just studied his son's face, seeing the ghost of Phalene in the pale gray eyes, that brown skin one shade darker than his own, the delicate angle of his jaw. Pel himself was on the stocky side, an ex-guard with the build to match. The only thing his son had was his nose, strong and prominent on a thin and elegant face that hardly matched it. His body was much the same; he was strong enough to help out in the bar and little more. Phalene had been that way, too, and Pel, with his natural bulk, couldn't really understand how that must feel in an argument like this—he'd never make it a physical fight, but he'd also never had to deal with the inherent intimidation of it either.

"I'm not denying it," Pel said finally, carefully

neutral.

Somehow, that made things worse with Bruant, like the fury that bobbed to the surface was pulled down by a stronger undertow of distress. "How many innocents have you handed over?"

Pel focused his gaze on his knuckles, tight on his mop, carefully swallowing his first reaction. "I don't know," he said. "Hopefully none."

"*Hopefully*," Bruant said. "That's the best you can do? The Inquisition hasn't given you numbers?"

"The Inquisition has said that all the ones I reported on were guilty," Pel said.

"You know that's impossible."

He knew.

Pel sighed roughly, feeling the force of it rough in his throat. "What do you want me to say, Bru? I'm not sorry. This is how this city remains safe. This is how I've kept *you* safe. We don't want to go to war again against *monsters*. We tried negotiation a long, long time ago, and you know what it got us? Dead civilians."

"This gets you dead civilians, too," Bruant muttered, hunched around his arm. At least he was keeping his voice down. "Do you think it doesn't, Dad? Anyone who acts in any way people don't expect, the Inquisition views as a threat. And you help them. Do you really expect me to join in on that?"

"If you want to take over the inn after me, the Inquisition will want its due." The anger inside him was welling more, brimming at the bottom of his throat, so every time he swallowed, every time he breathed, he could feel it hot inside him. Still, he only held onto the broom. He didn't move at all. "I told you that I help them because I thought you'd understand."

Bruant shrugged his jacket off violently, struggling

to do it one-armed, throwing it at the peg and missing. There was indeed some kind of bundle, Pel noticed with that detached part of him that noticed everything, clutched in that other arm, protected by his body. Bruant just looked at the jacket on the floor briefly, then bent and hung it up properly, seeming almost more annoyed at himself that he was doing so.

"You thought I'd understand," Bruant said finally, still facing away, staring at the coat rack. "I'll tell you what I *understand*. I understand that you've spilled blood to protect me. I don't want that, and I won't do it."

That was it. Pel shoved the mop back into its corner with such force that it clattered to the floor and took the broom with it. "You should *understand* that I do this to stop people like your mother from dying!" He only just managed to keep it from becoming a shout; the words came out with force regardless. "Demons are *beasts*, Bruant. They're godsdamned fucking monsters who exist to feed off us. Whether it's blood or fear or sex or anything else, they eat us." He shuddered, remembering how empty Phalene had been in the last hours. "That's all they want. And humans will let them do it, if they have a chance."

"Torturing humans ourselves is somehow *better*?" Bruant demanded. He spun to face Pel again, and Pel saw the small black bundle in his arms turn its head, gold eyes wide, one paw stretched up with its small white claws hooked in Bruant's shirt. "You're full of shit, Father!"

The argument carried him forward; asking about the animal would force them to both stop. "Yes, it's better!" Pel said. "I hate it, Bruant, I *hate* it, but it's up to people to behave in ways so that the Inquisition won't target them. Because we *have* to live this way. Anyone acting suspiciously might have had contact with one. Magicians will call them here. They have to be stopped. Anything to keep those monsters out of our city. I remember when we started to relax our standards. The demon your mother met seemed nice enough to her. Right until it got hungry, and then—"

Bruant adjusted his grip on the cat, cradling it gently even in his anger. "Don't you ever," he said, low but intense, hunched around his find again, his hair falling over his face and casting strange shadows on it in the light of the flickering candles overhead, "use my mother's death against me again. I have a right to be angry—my father's a murderer by proxy."

"Bruant—"

Stalking for the stairs, Bruant spat words like darts over his shoulder, "Innocent lives aren't worth shit to you. Humans kill each other just fine. Just look at you! You think you're actually doing something worthwhile. Wonder what everyone who got tortured because you ratted on them would have to say about that."

Pel sucked a breath in. When they'd first argued about it, Bruant had seemed shocked and angry but not—this. Not genuinely disgusted. Rage and fear churned around in Pel, a thick, sickening sludge that sat heavy on his stomach. Anger: He had thought Bruant would have understood, would have at least had *faith* even if he didn't. Terror: Bruant was all he had left. What if he couldn't forgive this?

I can't let this get to me. He forced himself to think that, forced himself to keep moving, not letting Bruant out of his sight as they moved up the stairs. *He has to understand.*

"Bruant! *Bruant*. Get back here." Pel followed him

all the way to his room, where Bruant was forced to stop just so he could get his key out and the door unlocked. He held out his hand between Bruant and the handle, palm open. "Look, I know you're angry, but you have to understand. I'm doing it to try to help others."

"I understand what you *think* you're doing," Bruant muttered through clenched teeth. The cat squirmed, and he ran a soothing hand down its back before using that hand to turn the knob.

Pel stared at the motion of Bruant's hand, how gentle it was despite his distress. "Fine," he said thickly. It was the closest he was going to get right now to any kind of resolution. "Now, care to explain what you're doing with that cat?"

"Giving it a home," Bruant said sharply.

"Bru—"

Bruant's gaze finally jerked up to his again. Those eyes, so much like his mother's, were equal parts guilt and anger, wild and so wide the whites were showing.

It's so hard, Pel thought helplessly, *for a child to be angry at his parent, even when he thinks he's in the right.* He had to remember that, too, and had to understand and forgive if he could expect even half of the same.

"I'm *lonely*," Bruant said. He'd probably only stopped himself from yelling it by the awareness that they had a guest staying only few rooms away. "I can save a street cat if I want to, can't I? I've been feeding it for weeks and it finally trusted me enough to come with me. Is that a problem, *Father*?"

What could he say to that? He opened his mouth, then closed it again wordlessly, letting his hand drop from between Bruant and the door.

The door was yanked open, and without saying anything else, Bruant stepped through and closed it behind himself.

"Fair enough," he answered finally, hoping that Bruant was still close enough to hear him.

Chapter Two

Pel got up at ten in the morning, a reasonable time considering the hours he always kept, to find that Bruant had already gone out. Pel checked his room, but there was no sign of either the boy or the cat. The window was open, so he could only assume the latter was off making its feline rounds.

Then again, Bruant was probably doing much the same. Avoiding work, roaming around to keep contact with his friends, retreading the old familiar streets with a new mindset.

Bruant would have to be more aware of the actual state of things now, Pel was sure. Every friend would be suspect. Bruant would find himself watching for their behavior and trying to decide if they were innocents. If they were Inquisition agents. If they were demon-touched. Knowing that the city was *safe* was a child's mindset. Knowing that people *kept* it that way was an adult's.

Knowing that it wasn't just the Inquisition who did it but your neighbors was a different type of experience altogether, and he regretted he'd had to be the one to give it to Bruant. It wasn't a great way to live. It was easy to be afraid of everyone. You couldn't know when you'd be the one to raise flags you hadn't even noticed.

After Phalene's death, the Inquisition had first approached him with the opportunity to prevent similar tragedies. He remembered the pain of trying to transition from the assumption that all his neighbors were trustworthy. He hadn't known what to do at first. He'd wandered around in a daze, looking at people and knowing that the world was split: Those who might collude with demons, those who might report the former, and those with little idea how fraught it all was. And him, moving from one group to another.

Pel pushed Bruant's window open wider and slid himself out it and onto the roof tiles outside, clucking his tongue to call for Bruant's cat. He scanned the horizon, glancing across the nearby rooftops; his inn was taller than most of the surrounding buildings, making it easy to see a good ways across the city, but trying to spot a cat in whatever chimney shadow it was hiding in was nearly impossible.

Still, he tried. It'd be harder for Bruant if his cat went missing after all this, and as fearless as cats were about heights, it wasn't like it was actually safe up here. He hadn't cleaned the moss from the roof for—

How long has it been since I came out here for anything but clearing out the eaves? he wondered suddenly. He'd had to repair some broken tiles a few years ago, he remembered, and there was the time he'd needed to remove a squirrel nest from his chimney. But he hadn't gone climbing around either time, and even then, he'd only been out here for work.

He used to come out on the rooftop with Phalene, during the day or at night after the bar closed. He'd proposed to her out here, late at night with the stars brilliant in the sky, the two of them lying back and making up stories about the constellations—Phalene's favorite hobby. She'd always fantasized about there being more to the world than there was. He'd described one of the constellations as being like a ring, glittering with gems, and when she turned to him grinning, he'd been holding the real ring out.

They'd made love up here that night, her father one floor below, and he'd surprised them right after by coming into her room. She'd had to come back in through the window and pretend to have been alone, while he climbed down the wall. He'd dropped the last ten feet and sprained his ankle.

Pel shook his head, smiling around that old ache. It had been a hard injury to explain away to his commanding officer, and he'd set himself to practicing climbing the training wall in the practice field for ages to avoid having it happen again. He still kept it up whenever he hit the field, though just for pleasure these days. Not much call for an innkeeper to go scaling walls, and he didn't have anyone whose windows he'd climb out of.

The cat still hadn't turned up, though, and the ache was growing. No point dwelling, he reminded himself, and climbed back inside.

He kept the window slightly open as he left Bruant's room and locked the door behind himself. If Bruant wanted a cat, then he wasn't going to shut it out. He doubted that it'd come back on its own, regardless of how many weeks Bruant had been feeding it—it was just a street cat, after all—but that was Bruant's problem to deal with. All he could do was support him.

After that, he moved down the hall, rapping on Tari's door. "Need your room cleaned?" There was no answer, and he paused, considering his options. After the late and busy night she'd had, she might still be in the room, sleeping. *She's probably out, though. A traveler keeps sunlight hours.*

Pel didn't bother to second-guess himself again. He opened the door with his spare on his key chain. If she were in, he could always apologize and stick to his original excuse of coming in to clean. '*I thought you were out,*' would hardly be a lie.

Sure enough, the bed was empty, though she'd at least made it behind herself. The room smelled of sex regardless, an uncomfortably thick smell, and he opened the window as he searched.

She'd taken her travel bags with her. That by itself wasn't overly suspicious if she were trying to make a sale, though—she'd have to be able to check what she could ditch and what she'd need to resupply. But it made her harder to investigate; he searched around for any discarded clothes and found none.

Looks like she likes to keep things tidy. He supposed he could appreciate that.

'Nothing to report' was as good news as he was likely to get. No matter how angry Bruant was at him, it wasn't like he ever enjoyed having to pass his suspicions on to the Inquisition. Every time, there was the guilt. The fear that this time he'd condemned an innocent.

It was just that the risks of *not* doing so were too high.

He closed the window and let himself out of the room, then went to finish cleaning and get himself ready for the day.

~~*

Tari didn't return until it was starting to get dark, a couple of hours before the inn reopened for business, but he didn't expect her sooner as she'd have to get her midday meal out regardless; they didn't get enough patrons staying over to make it worthwhile to open for lunch, since most people worked through the day.

The cooks were due to show up to start getting food prepped, and he half expected to see one of them when he heard the door open. Seeing her instead was a strange shock. There was something incredibly physical about her, a presence that filled the room far beyond her actual size.

"Welcome back," he said, instantly smiling. "Enjoying the city?"

"Something like that." Tari shrugged but smiled back nonetheless. She came over to the seat nearest to where he was working and slung herself down, dropping the bag on the table. "Not much luck selling my goods. I was hoping things would go a little more smoothly."

It was said so lightly, so heedless of what it was actually like here, that he felt his stomach twist. "Well, you're a stranger."

The words just slipped out. He shouldn't be warning her at all—he knew that much. The Inquisition needed to be free to do what it had to without interference, if worst came to worst.

But what Bruant had said stuck with him, and maybe she deserved at least as much forewarning as anyone else in this damn city.

"What's that got to do with it?" she asked, her eyes fixed on him. "Most towns love traveling merchants."

"They don't know that your jewels aren't cursed or tainted," he explained, trying to keep his own tone light. "Owning that kind of thing puts the new owner at as much risk of being taken by the Inquisition as whoever sold it. Once a demon's influence has gotten onto something, it's there to stay."

Surprisingly, she laughed, tilting her head curiously and sending her hair tumbling over her shoulders. She looked at him from that angle, eyes even brighter than before. "Ah, so it's like that," she said. "But the guards let me in, so surely they all know I'm harmless? After that much questioning, I'd hope so."

"Sure," he said, "they deal with *blatant* intrusions. But if your business seems genuine, and you seem human to all their tests, they'll let you take shelter here. We're humans-first here, after all. They checked your belongings, right?"

"They did," she said. "For anything that was obviously some kind of enchantment." She tapped her forearm, hidden under a billowy sleeve. "And when they tested me, I bled red blood just like any other human."

"And they asked you questions about your history and your business to see if anything seemed off," he said, as agreeably as he could despite how raw he felt about this all over again. "So they won't keep you from entering."

She spread her hands, grinning. The whole situation seemed to almost be delighting her, and his frustration welled up more thoroughly.

This isn't a game. People die.

"Then what's the problem?" she asked lightly. "I passed the tests. If I'm not human, your guards failed at their job."

"Yeah, and that's why people aren't buying what you're selling." It came out snappish. "There are things that can get around wards. Possession, something riding around in the back of your mind. A slow-acting curse. Demon-borne perversions and inhuman desires—"

"You make it sound so appealing, sir," she murmured in her husky voice.

Why wouldn't she take this seriously? She didn't realize the risk, that much was clear. He'd been working with the Inquisition long enough that he could tell an inquisitor that he suspected her, and she'd vanish just like *that*. She sounded so well-traveled—did she really not know what could happen? If she talked about demonic influence this lightly to the wrong person, it would be the last stop on her travels.

"People will test you in all kinds of ways. I think you should mind yourself a little better."

Whether it was the shortness of his tone or something else about what he'd said, she seemed to sober a little. Her smile faded, though her eyes seemed to grow more interested, intense and focused. If he didn't know the thought were insane, he'd think she was *intrigued* by the risk.

"Really," she said. "That's unnerving. But surely it's not as bad as all that?"

"It happens often enough." Pel reached for an example he *hadn't* been involved in, too sore to think about the ones he had been. "There was an old woman recently, Vautour. She used to come eat here sometimes. Well, she was getting older and she told her friends and neighbors about how afraid she was that she'd pass on soon."

Tari tilted her head. "A reasonable fear. Certainly one more human than demonic."

"Sure, but the more she talked about it, the more it sounded to people like she was looking for ways to stop it. Medicines, serums, those can treat the symptoms, but mortality is the human condition. Ultimately there's no way to permanently stop humans from dying. Age has its way with all of us." He leaned against the wall, crossing his arms. At least she seemed to be taking it seriously now. "Not quite true, actually. There's one way."

"Ah," Tari said, unsmiling. "I begin to see."

"If she wanted a power like that... if she had the potential for magic, she could become a magician." He hesitated, then corrected himself. "Or she'd pretty much *need* to become one eventually, is what I've heard—it's like they can't help themselves. And even if she didn't have that power, she could still sell her soul. Either way, though, she'd be looking for ways to consort with demons. Once that became a reasonable fear and the Inquisition heard about it, she got taken away. I heard they had to drag her down the street screaming. People talked more about the scene she caused than the lady herself."

Tari was silent. She closed her eyes, resting her chin on her closed fist, as if imagining the scenario, playing it out in her mind. He studied her face, finding it odd to see her without that constant smirk. "And what will they do to her?" she asked finally. "To some old lady whose worst crime was to be afraid of dying. Probably harmless. You know, that, right?"

Pel suddenly found himself glad their eye contact had broken. "Probably," he agreed. "I don't know what'll happen," he added shortly, though he suspected he was lying. "If she confesses, it'll be a quick death. If she doesn't, they'll try to find proof before running her out."

"Torture."

"Interrogation. She could be proven innocent," he said, though his tone sounded unconvincing even to his own ears. "That doesn't tend to happen, though. The Inquisition is confident in who they take *before* they snatch them up."

Tari's eyes opened again. What he saw in them took him aback: she was still amused. *Why? By my reaction to her?* Or was it just some kind of black humor to deal with the situation?

"Lovely," Tari said dryly. "She was afraid of dying so she gets a choice between a quick death or an agonizing one? That's not really my scene, just so you know, torture and death."

The conversation felt stifling, a sharp reminder of the way Bruant had looked at him after they'd had the same one. "It's ultimately to protect the city. Demons do try to get in here sometimes, because there's so many humans. To them, it's an insult. A safe zone for prey. So of course they want to sneak in, feast, and then sneak back out after glutting themselves."

"Wow." Tari's eyes widened with faux concern. "You seem to have a real clear idea of what demons are thinking and feeling. Careful that the Inquisition doesn't target you for that one."

"That's—"

The door opened again, and he turned, relieved by the interruption of what surely must be the cooks finally arriving. The feeling vanished at once as Bruant entered the hall, though he seemed in a tamer mood today, quiet and slightly guilty as he met Pel's eyes. His hair, wind tangled, hid part of his expression.

Tari, seeing Pel's attention shift, turned as well. They both watched as Bruant ducked his head to avoid eye contact and headed up to his room in silence. The little black cat trotted close at his heels, vanishing with Bruant.

"Interesting," Tari said, once Bruant was out of earshot. "*There's* something you don't see every day."

Pel sighed. "Yeah," he said, and scrubbed a hand through his short-cropped hair. The change of subject was a relief. "I don't know how he got that cat to like him so much. Strays are usually pretty skittish."

"Well, if he fed it often enough," Tari said, "I think it'd get attached. Most creatures feel that way."

"You mean it knows where its next meal is coming from," Pel said. "Cats aren't exactly known for getting attached."

Tari laughed, low and soft. "You think that makes a difference?" She tilted her head as if she were stretching her neck, like she needed to buy time to figure out how to put something. "If it's coming indoors this easily, it's not feral. It was probably abandoned by someone who used to take care of it, right?"

"I guess?"

"So it doesn't have a colony. Which means it's lonely. It's probably scared. Even if it's surviving fine on its own—" it had looked healthy enough, after all, with clear eyes and sleek black coat, "—the rules it used to live by changed in some way. It needs people, or at least company, but it doesn't have a sense of who's safe." She chuckled, resting her chin on her fist. "Cats aren't actually as solitary as people think, you know. They're quite social. The fact they're predators, or that they hunt alone, doesn't change that."

Pel shrugged. "I guess," he repeated awkwardly. "It's not like I know that much about cats."

"Well, that's why most ferals have colonies. And

why pet cats *do* bond," she said lightly. "It's not just food. There's a social need there that needs to be met. So assume someone came along and started caring for it and paying it attention. Even a scared stray cat might come indoors for that."

It did all sound reasonable. "Following at his heels, though?" Pel asked. "That's some needy cat."

"Sure is," Tari said, and laughed again, quiet. "Sort of nice to see, though, especially when you start going on about how dangerous this place is. Warms the heart."

"It's not dangerous to *cats*."

"Sweetheart," Tari said, "any place that's dangerous to people is dangerous to pets."

Fair enough. People who vanished might have pets that ended up on the streets. Paranoia over familiars might put any stray at risk. It wasn't something he heard of happening generally, but he could see how it might arise.

"Well," Pel confessed, "as long as it makes Bruant happier, he could adopt half the strays around here and I wouldn't complain."

"Mmm. He did seem kind of upset yesterday," Tari said, prompting.

He opened his mouth to respond, then felt a shock run through him at how easily he'd reacted to her. He felt himself on the edge of slipping, saying too much—that maybe he'd *already* said too much in the aftermath of fighting with Bruant, of remembering Phalene, of all the rest. "He did," he said flatly.

For a moment, Tari just looked at him.

Then she grinned again, a rakish look at odds with her delicate face. "I think I'll talk to him," she said. As Pel began to bristle and opened his mouth to protest, she added, "*Not* about you, don't worry about that. But if you've never had a cat, he won't know how to take care of them. I can give him some tips. Maybe it'll cheer him up."

Pel let his breath out slowly. *Why does it feel like some kind of trap?* The thought was absurd. He couldn't just forbid her from talking to his son, not without seeming suspicious about it. And Bruant wouldn't tell her anything about him. Even angry, he'd put his father first, Pel was sure of that.

Still. "You could tell me, too," Pel said. "If the cat's going to be part of my household now, I should know—"

Tari held up a hand. "You know, I'm going to stop you there, sweetheart," she said, ignoring the flat look he gave her at the pet name. Maybe she could tell he was a little flattered despite himself. "If the kiddo and you are fighting, he's not going to be happy about you stepping in to take his responsibilities away from him. He picked that cat up, right? If *he* wants to tell you how to help take care of *his* cat, that's one thing. Not my place to start giving you tips."

Irritation welled up. It was just a damn cat. Anyone could take care of it, and it was more than a little likely that he'd *have* to some days. And Bruant had always shared everything with him, always told him everything.

But—

She was right. Bruant had learned something that made him have to reevaluate his father. Bruant was old enough to strike out on his own in little ways. Bruant was struggling in a way that Pel *couldn't* take part in. Maybe Bruant needed things of his own now he could keep secret, the same way he'd started needed his space as he got older.

All he could do was try to help Bruant understand him, and offer whatever understanding he could in return.

"All right," he said finally. "But only about the cat, you hear? Don't get into my argument with him, even if he brings it up. That's something *I* have to work out with *him*."

"Me?" she asked, smiling winningly and flattening a hand on her chest. "I would never."

~~*

It was hard to fight the urge to eavesdrop, but that would *definitely* be crossing his son's boundaries. He fought the unkind urge as best as he could, put his head down, and focused on his work. He had a damn business to run, and he was determined to stick to just that—his business.

He soon found that it was easy enough to do. The cooks showed up only a little while later, he got the bar ready for the day, and he kept himself as focused as he could on the work in front of him instead of what was going on overhead.

To his surprise, only Furt showed up, sulking his way down to his usual bar stool.

"Your brother busy today?" Pel asked.

"Spent too much time with booze and sex yesterday," Furt said. "Rolled home exhausted after dawn. Even *he* decided to take a break for tonight."

Pel snorted. "Good news for you, hm?"

"I'm not here for my brother's sloppy seconds," Furt said, but interest sparked in his eyes regardless. "She not here today?"

"She's here, but not down yet."

That was, of course, the moment Tari decided to make her reappearance. She exited the stairwell with more energy than elegance, thumping down the stairs and grinning widely.

"Hey!" she called to the crowd. "Who missed me?"

The question got several cheers in response; it seemed that she didn't *need* elegance. She bowed dramatically to the couple of people already in the bar, then made a beeline for Furt's table and laughed as she sank down across from him.

Guess that's just what she's like. He kept expecting something more refined and stately out of her, and couldn't say why. Tari was rowdy and ready for excitement. It was Phalene who would have swept down quietly and comfortably, nodding to everyone in familiar fondness—

I really wish I could unthink that.

He threw himself into his work again.

~~*

Halfway through the evening, Tari went up to her room with Furt. She didn't come back down until after closing, and she did so alone, but the evidence of their activities was clear. She was barefoot, her pants hanging loose around her hips, and her plain men's shirt, normally tucked in and styled up with her vest, was untucked and unbuttoned past her collarbone. Pel was sure he would be seeing the swell of a breast if she had any swell to speak of.

"Need any help?" she asked, her voice soft.

Well, she sure seems satisfied, he thought with some unexpected bitterness. Her eyes were hazy, lips plumper than he remembered them being. "No," he said shortly. And then, relenting a little—she *was* a guest, and the offer *had* seemed to be in a good enough spirit—he added, "I couldn't ask a patron to help clean. Usually Bruant does, but..." He trailed off. She'd seen too much of their family drama already.

"Well. Children who have become adults have their own set of concerns," Tari said. She seemed lazily pleased somehow. "I doubt that right now he wants things to continue like they always have."

"You're probably right," he admitted. "I guess I'll have to look into hiring help."

She snorted indelicately. "Talk to him first, or you'll offend him by not giving him the option."

"Ah, but is there any way *not* to offend him these days?" he asked dryly.

For some reason, Tari seemed to take that seriously. She watched him with curious eyes for long enough he grew uncomfortable and turned back to his work.

From behind him, she said, belatedly, "You're probably caught up in what he means to you. Perhaps spend some time thinking of what he means to himself."

He clenched his jaw a little. Of course he was thinking of Bruant. Nobody thought about Bruant as much as he did. "Right," he said.

When he didn't say anything else, she sighed. "I'll be heading back upstairs, then," she said. She moved to the stairs, then hesitated. "I'll be staying here longer than a few days, I think. I have enough to pay for my room, but I'm having trouble making enough on top of that to manage traveling without, as you said, earning the townsfolks' trust. All right?"

"However long you need the room," he muttered.

"Thanks, sweetheart," Tari said.

Pel didn't relax until the sound of bare feet on the stairs receded.

Chapter Three

Almost a week passed and Tari's declaration of "longer than a few days" didn't become more specific in that time. She seemed fine with it—maybe too fine, Pel thought, given the circumstances. But she was having fun. She fell somewhere between sleazy and easy, but not in a bad way; if she were a man, he'd consider her a rake. She clearly enjoyed both the crowds of the public room and the privacy of a bedroom, but she was also genuinely good company. He could understand why people were so drawn to her.

He liked having her there. And her money was good. But it was a situation that couldn't go on indefinitely, and the thought preyed more on his mind as each day passed.

Hoping to talk with her, he knocked on Tari's door midday and was a little surprised when she was actually inside to accept.

"Come in!" she called.

She was dressed down again, breeches and partially unbuttoned shirt, but it was considerably less uncomfortable to see when she wasn't immediately post-coital. She sat on the bed and looked attentive as he leaned against the wall, crossing his arms.

"Is there a problem?" she asked.

Pel realized how he must look and tried to relax. "No, it's fine," he said. "It's about your stay here, but

I'm not going to kick you out—"

Tari let out an exaggerated breath of relief, then laughed. "You looked so serious."

"Not on—my behalf," he stammered, finding himself going a little red. Flustered, not sure why his pulse was racing, he pushed on. "I was thinking about your situation. Your goal is to make enough money trading in gems for cash that you can restock your supplies properly, correct?"

"Correct," she said. "And that hasn't happened. But I do still have enough keep paying you."

He nodded slowly. "I don't want you to arrive in a new town broke," he said finally. "If you need to restock there and are out of jewels, what then?"

"Usually I don't need to restock that often," she began. Her shoulders rose as she seemed to get a little defensive.

He considered that. Her gaze was lowered, and for once her expression had gone stiff. It was hard to say how much of the defensiveness might be for a reason, how much her lack of care for how this situation was dragging on could be due to no actual need for money. A demonic contract, or something similar.

It was easy to think that way. It was *habit* to think that way. But he was well aware of how hard he'd worked to get through to her so she'd have some fear of strangers in this place. It was much, much more likely that her defensiveness was simply from being called out in any way after that discussion. The fact that she knew that something that small *could* be suspicious.

Pel let out a breath through his nose. "I have a long-term rate," he said, hearing it come out too abrupt. "Normally I wouldn't offer it to someone who was here for as short a time as you, but 'indefinite' is a pretty long time."

Her pale eyes widened. It was, he thought abruptly, the first time he'd caught her off guard. That by itself was a strange realization. Pel wasn't used to seeing someone who was that confident almost all the time, even if it made sense—in her line of business, and with the risks she took traveling around and visiting demon-occupied cities, she'd have to be sure of herself.

"I... are you certain?" she asked finally. "I don't want your business to hurt because I'm here."

"I'm sure," he said firmly, trying to absorb that usual confidence and reflect it back at her until she picked it up again. "Consider it an exchange for you helping with Bru."

That in itself was worth more than the extra income would bring in. *Shit, it's priceless.* As much as he hated to admit it, a near-stranger had helped his son more than he could. Things had been different since she'd gone in and talked to him about the cat—

Kip, Bruant had told him. He'd named it Kip.

And she hadn't just talked to him the once. She'd gone in to see him a few times, short chats and casual visits. Pel suspected they were talking about more than the cat in there, that they were discussing some part of the real thing that was bothering Bruant. Pel could only hope, only believe, that if it had to do with *him*, Bruant was deliberately unspecific. He didn't think his son would say anything about his role with the Inquisition. He hoped, too, that Tari honored the request he'd made, didn't ask and refused to hear talk of Pel.

Well, whatever they're talking about, it seems to

be doing the trick. He was sure, too, that they were just talking. Tari's exuberance for intimacy aside, he didn't believe she'd sleep with his son. She seemed to respect the difficulties between them and he couldn't imagine her doing anything that might deliberately make it worse.

Bruant seemed calmer, if that was the proper word for the secretive happiness that Pel kept seeing on his face. It didn't seem quite right; there was still a constant energy, a constant tension, around him. But neither that angry air nor the cloud of guilt seemed to follow him around anymore. Actually, the only thing following him these days was Kip, tagging along more like a baby duck or a love-struck suitor than a cat.

Bruant still went out for most of the day, and still wasn't really talking to Pel about much of anything, but even if he seemed to enjoy having secrets from Pel, he was helping with chores again. Being around him.

Not picking a fight at every opportunity.

Tari had been considering the offer, still looking down. Her face had softened in some indefinable way. "I haven't done much."

"Well, whatever you've done," Pel said, still firm, "it's made a difference to *him*. Besides, it's nice to have a woman around the place again."

He regretted saying that immediately.

The comment startled her out of the strange, vulnerable mood she'd been in. Her head jerked up, expression almost incredulous before she burst into a laugh. "Is that how you feel?" she said. "I got the impression from Bruant that it had been a long time since your wife passed. You asked me a while ago if I were looking for a husband. I hope that doesn't mean you were looking for a wife."

That struck a nerve that he hadn't even realized was still raw. It hit him with such intensity that he felt dizzy rather than any specific emotion—not angry, not hurt, just *off guard*. He drew a breath in, unsteady. "No, I—no."

"I'm sorry to say, but I'm not marriageable material. I know that well enough."

Well, she was open enough about her habits, and there was no way she'd think he was unaware of them. It was almost a relief to think about that than the rest of it. *Is she turning tricks in the room?* he wondered. *Is that why she's so sure she won't run out of money, or why she brings so many people up?* The thought did make some sense, but he dismissed it almost at once. He would have noticed if any business were being conducted at the bar, and neither the regulars nor Tari seemed the sort to expect that sort of thing to get worked out after the fact.

It was simply pleasure.

He floundered to find the line of conversation again. "It's not—I wasn't looking to *marry* you for it. I just meant that you're helping Bru in a way I can't. He hasn't had a feminine influence in his life for a very long time."

"I don't think that's gender," Tari said gently. "I think you're just too close to the situation. But that's to be expected. You two have spent all your time together as your only family for just as long."

"Well—" He raised his eyes to hers again and found her watching him with an almost coy look, eyelids half-lowered. The expression sent a rush of heat through him and made his words dry up.

Tari noticed. "But *you're* reacting to me with that

sense of 'having a woman around the place', whether or not *he* is," she said, still coy. "Am I being a feminine influence on *you*?"

And if the earlier comment had struck a nerve, that was like a bucket of ice water. "If you're asking if you're like my wife—no," he said, hoarse. She was still attractive, still appealing, but... "Nothing like."

"Tell me about her," Tari said. She grabbed a pillow from the bed and hugged it, grinning up at him like a child waiting for story time.

He drew a sharp breath to refuse, hurt and off-kilter, and something he'd told Bruant came back to mind: *the more people remember her, the longer her memory will live.* He let his breath out between his teeth in a slow hiss of air. "Not much to say," he said, hesitating.

"How did you two meet?" Tari asked, still smiling at him, heavy-eyed.

Pelerin closed his eyes, like he could redefine the space around them by doing so. The room itself was his, of course. His building, his rooms. But it felt heavy with Tari's overwhelming presence, like he was the stranger who didn't belong there.

When he opened them, nothing had changed.

"I used to be a city guard," he said slowly. "When I was younger, I mean. I joined in my teens. It's mostly the older guards who work the gates so I never ended up on that kind of interrogation duty. Since I was younger and fit, I mostly worked in the city streets, doing patrols."

Tari gave him an obvious once-over. "I could see that."

Strangely embarrassed, he made a face. How long had it been since anyone had properly flirted with him, even if just to tease? He didn't know how to respond, and pushed on. "It wasn't a dramatic story, how we met. Phalene's father ran the inn. I drank here often enough after work, and she served a lot of the food. We hit it off, got together, and I withdrew from the guard and took over running the inn when her father passed. She taught me how the business worked. We'd been together a couple of years when she had Bruant."

"What was she like?"

"That's the part that's nothing like you," he said, trying not to be unkind about it and hearing his voice come out maybe too soft instead. It was impossible to excise the fond tone though, as memories came so clearly that Pel expected Phalene could open the door and walk in right then. The shape of her face, the way the light caught her dark eyes, her ever-smiling soft mouth, the scent of her hair.

"She was a lot less down-to-earth," he went on. "She liked to dream about life outside the city. She was kind of... fascinated, I suppose, with what it would be like to be a human living among demons. The fantasy thrilled her. She was like that in every way, though—driven by fantasy, I mean. She was always wanting to try something new, experience the world. It's why she loved the inn so much, getting to hear all kinds of people's stories."

"Sounds more like me than you realize," Tari said, and laughed.

He smiled at the clear tone of it but could feel a chill settling into his stomach. "I..." he began, then quieted, helpless as the memories became darker.

"Pel?"

"She died," he said finally. Then, knowing Tari already knew that, he added, "It was because of that curiosity. The city watch relaxed over the years due to a lack of incidents. Nothing had happened since long before either of us were born, so it was easy to go in and out of Dolana, back then. She went out of the city to gather some wildflowers for the tables and met a... person out there. It would later turn out to be an aluga. She told me about the stranger she had met, a friendly woman with eyes that were black even where the whites should be. Talked to her about the weather, nothing important. I didn't think it was worth mentioning to anyone."

"And?" It didn't seem like Tari needed an explanation as to what an aluga was. Pel had, back then, even if he'd never forget now. They passed for human in everything but their solid black eyes, until they attacked and their natures became clearer: demons who fed on human pain and fear.

"What do you think?" Pel said flatly. "The third time they met, it fed. Her scream was too late to bring the guards in time to save her from the attack. She died slowly over hours, in terror and agony." He forced himself to draw a breath despite how tight his lungs felt. "We did a hunt and caught the demon, though."

"I imagine that did not go well for the demon," Tari said, her tone light but expression serious.

"Who the hell cares about the demon? It kept the rest of the village safe," Pel said roughly. An outsider couldn't understand. "It helped us test some of the methods the Inquisition had studied to try to trap or harm demons. They gave me the honor of using it to kill her."

"Ah," Tari breathed, watching him almost with caution now.

That's a normal response, he thought, depressed

and hurting. Normal to be cautious of someone whose grief ended in vengeance. Normal to be wary of someone who admitted to having tortured and killed something, even if it was a demon, the demon that had killed his wife.

He looked back up at Tari, and was surprised to see that her expression was still odd. Sympathetic, but with something underlying it. Interest still, maybe. Some kind of fascination. "I'm sorry for your loss," she said softly.

Suddenly, facing her was too painful. "I should... I should go. He cleared his throat and pushed away from the wall. "I've brought the mood down enough. I'll charge you the long-term rate from now on."

"Thank you," Tari said. And then, in a strange, pleased tone, "And thank you for sharing that with me. I know it must have been hard. I appreciate it."

He glanced back at her, saw that bright-eyed look still on her face, and just shook his head as he left the room.

The expression was familiar—*too* familiar. It was how Phalene had gotten about people's stories, even the tragic ones.

Just hearing about the wide range of experiences in human life had interested her so much. Someone else's horrible adventures, stories that had nothing to do with her.

~~*

The next afternoon, Pel heard voices coming from Bruant's room and assumed that Tari was in there—but five steps past Bruant's door, he stopped cold.

Tari had gone out earlier to keep pushing a

business deal. He was *sure* she hadn't come back yet.

Pel stood tense where he was, trapped in a parent's indecisive horror. *Bruant's an adult now.* If he had a girl over, that was his right—or, for that matter, a boy; Pel himself had dated a few when he was younger.

But Bruant hadn't mentioned being interested in anyone to him before, and when he'd passed by Pel on his way upstairs earlier, he'd been alone. The front door was still shut to anyone who didn't have a key, so either he'd somehow missed Bruant smuggling someone past him, which would already be a concern, because *why*, or someone had come in through the window.

And *that* sort of behavior, happening on the second floor, still in (albeit dimming) daylight, was more likely to be demonic than human. Sure, it was possibly normal—he'd done it himself, after all—but cubants like incubi and succubi were famous for it. And surely there were other types of demons who could do likewise. There seemed to be more variety of the monsters out there than names he knew for them.

It's probably fine, he told himself. *It's probably nothing.*

But he'd be fucked if he'd let something happen to someone he loved a second time. Anxious, fretting, he turned and walked back to Bruant's room. The sound was still there, muffled and indistinct. He'd have to put his ear up to the door to hear details, and if it were just a lover, that'd be a horrible violation of Bruant's privacy.

Indecision gripped him briefly, and then he forced himself to *make* a decision. He wouldn't listen. He wouldn't throw the door open. He wouldn't do anything that he wouldn't have wanted done to him back in the day.

But he still needed to know.

So he knocked.

Immediately the sound stopped. There was a silence, as if Bruant—and perhaps, whoever was in there with him—was waiting to see if he'd leave.

Shit. He knocked again. "Bru—?"

This time, he could hear Bruant's voice through the door, raised to carry: "One minute, Dad!"

He strained to hear what was happening, but didn't hear anything now. *What should I do?*

Bruant's locked turned with an audible click. It was too soon for his window to have been opened and closed to let someone out; he must have got up from wherever he was and come right over. It didn't entirely reassure Pel—he still had no idea what exactly he was going to see when the door opened—but it was still a damn sight better than the alternative.

But when it creaked open, Bruant not bothering to keep it closed but pulling it wide, all he saw was Bruant himself, shirtless and staring out at him in wide-eyed alarm from his perfectly normal messy room with its unmade bed and its unfortunate pile of laundry on the floor. "Dad? What is it?"

Pel looked past him, searching the room for anything unusual, but there didn't seem to be anyone or anything there except Kip, sitting up on Bruant's bed and looking curious about the commotion.

"Dad?" Bruant prompted again, brows furrowed.

Maybe I'm losing it. "I thought I heard... I thought I heard you talking to someone."

Bruant stared at him, keeping himself almost unnaturally still, then abruptly stepped aside, holding his door open. "I was talking to Kip," he said slowly and strained, like he wasn't sure when his father had turned into a madman.

"To Kip," Pel repeated blankly. He looked at the cat, who blinked back slowly, then flopped down as if it had tired of these shenanigans. "And... was the cat answering back?"

"What?" Bruant's voice pitched up a bit, cracking. "That's crazy, Dad. What the hell? He's a *cat*! Cats can't talk."

Pel found himself embarrassed at the incredulity in Bruant's tone. "That's—no. I *know* that. I mean, I thought I heard two voices. Is that something you can explain, Bru?"

"Maybe you heard his meowing as another voice?" Bruant asked slowly, tense and uncomfortable, staring at Pel with the near panic of talking to someone who was acting completely unreasonable. "I was trying to teach him tricks. You didn't hear any *words*, did you...?"

"No," Pel admitted, hearing his voice come out just as embarrassed as he felt. "Just two different tones."

Bruant let out a short, sharp breath. He blinked rapidly, looking down as relief washed over his features. "Way to freak me out, Dad," he said. Then, seeming to perk up instantly in a surprising mood swing, "Look, it's normal with him. I'll show you. Kip. Hey, Kip."

The cat flicked an ear in their direction but didn't move.

"*Kip.*"

Finally, Kip lifted his head, letting out a low-voiced complaint. "*Mow.*"

The smile Bruant gave Pel was almost eager, like

he thought he was in trouble and wanted to please. "He does that if I talk to him. He likes to chat back. Kip, who's a good cat?"

Kip's tail thumped on the bed a few times in agitation. "Mooooow," he whined back.

"Kip, will you sit? Sit, Kip!"

"Meeeeeeeeehh." The cat was answering again but very definitely was not sitting, still flopped bonelessly on his side.

Bruant grinned at Kip, then turned the smile on Pel. Bruant's anxiety had faded into something softer and more genuine, and Pel had to admit that it had been a while since he'd seen his son look at him with that kind of happiness. "Getting him to actually do the trick is the hard part," Bruant admitted. "Anyway, you think that might be what you heard?"

It had been pretty muffled. It really could have been something as simple and stupid as a cat meowing back. Pel put his face in his hands, groaning. "I don't even know what I was thinking."

"You've been stressed lately," Bruant said consolingly. He seemed to hesitate, then took two quick steps over, put a hand on Pel's back, and patted it awkwardly a few times. "My fault."

"No, you... like you said, you had the right to be angry," Pel muttered into his hands. He scrubbed at his face, trying to will his embarrassment down. His protectiveness and fear had been suffocating; what they had turned into almost felt more so. "It's all right if you're angry with me. I mean, I don't like it, but..."

Bruant's hand paused in its movement on his back. "Thanks," he said, and there was a guilty tone in his voice again that was horrible to hear. "I appreciate that."

Chapter Four

When Pel saw Tari in the late afternoon the next day, he told her what had happened, expecting to get a laugh out of her.

He'd managed to calm down sometime after he'd excused himself. It had almost taken to the start of the work day, so he focused as always on the cooks, the food, the regulars, the daily work. When the day was over, he'd collapsed into bed for a night of nonsensical stress dreams.

The next day, he did usual morning routine: he woke up, finished cleaning, and went for his daily jog. The jog itself wasn't enough to reduce his stress, so he hit up the training field. Publicly available, it was his favorite place to work out and go a few round with some old friends from the guard. He climbed the wall, focusing on nothing but finding his next handholds and footholds, and thought he'd sweated it out.

He hadn't. He kept thinking of that scene, and how humiliating it was, inevitably drawn back to the topic of his own neurotic behavior.

By then, it had become funny to him. *I deserve a laugh at that kind of paranoia*, he'd decided. Somehow, his fear had crept up on him and become so large that he'd literally jumped into a situation where the rational explanation should have occurred to him without needing to bother Bruant at all.

He wasn't expecting Tari to stare at him, looking

genuinely discomfited.

"Tari...?" he asked, suddenly embarrassed again. This time, it was less for his actual behavior and more about how it might be perceived. What if it wasn't funny? There was a good chance he was actually starting to look deranged to others. He'd been tossing around thoughts of paranoia and neuroses all day—what was to stop someone else from doing the same?

"Well," she said finally. "I'm glad it turned out to be nothing, Pel. But what if it *had* been a demon?"

He blinked. The thought had become so absurd to him that it took a moment to pull himself back to that moment of fear, without the shadow of ridicule overlaying it. "What?"

"If you had unlocked the door and thrown it open, and found Bru sitting there talking with a demon," Tari said. "What would you have done?"

"I'd have—" It took him a moment to realize both his error of the day before and his need not to mention it. He had an amulet, given to him by the Inquisition for his service with the aluga, which could briefly bind a demon. It was a rare thing, inherited from a magician who had passed through before, and stronger than the wards the guards used to test visitors to see if they flinched. He could have used that to trap it, but he hadn't been carrying it around with him regularly for years. He hadn't even *thought* about it for years.

"Well," he said, searching for another answer to give even as he spoke. "I'd have run the demon off. If it was sitting and talking with him, it would probably rather not have to fight. I'd run it off, and then I'd make sure Bruant was safe. I'd pay the Inquisition to check the place out, tell them about the near miss. They wouldn't need to know he'd been talking to it. He'd be safe and it would get properly hunted."

"Sure," she said. "From what I've heard, that'd be fine... if it were an *unwanted* demon intrusion. No humans to blame for that one. But if they were sitting and talking, what if the demon was there with Bruant's consent?"

"There's no such thing," he said shortly. "Not really. They can convince people otherwise, but that doesn't mean it's true."

She lifted her brows. "Those are some fine hairs to split," she said dryly. "Speaking as someone who comes from a place where humans and demons interact all the time, I'd say that a human still has a choice about whether or not they want to talk to a specific demon."

"They might think they do, but—"

"And you think they don't. What makes you right and them wrong?"

"It's—because they're demons—"

Tari sighed. She flopped back on her bed and spread her arms out. Pel, sitting next to her, found himself caught in the strangely pleasant position of looking down at her. The thought of leaning down to kiss her flitted through his mind, but it was quickly pushed away; the mood wasn't right. Not to mention how inappropriate it would be, as her landlord.

It didn't make him want it less.

For a few moments, Tari just lay there before speaking again. "If you're wrong, your world view might just fall apart, I'm sure. But maybe it doesn't matter. It's sort of beside the point, isn't it? So let's get back to that. If, last night, there was a demon there, one who Bruant *wanted* there, what would you do?"

All he could do was stare at her. "He wouldn't," he

said. "Bruant wouldn't do that. He knows what happened to his mother."

"A human being whose mother was killed by another human being might, someday, hold conversations with an unrelated human being," Tari pointed out, strangely caustic.

"We aren't talking about humans," Pel told her, hearing his voice come out more stunned than offended. "Maybe you've been blinded to the problem since you used to live with demons, but if you spend your time with only humans for a while, I think you'll see the difference."

"Like I said," Tari said, flapping a hand above herself in the air, "this isn't about our world views right now. Stop changing the subject. What would you do if it happened?"

His heart was stuttering, leaving an uneven feeling in his chest and tension knotting his stomach. He'd imagined Bruant in Phalene's place often enough. When Bruant had still been a child, Pel's nightmares were of Bruant's tiny body as often as they were of Phalene.

I don't want to think about this.

But, with Tari's gaze fixed on him, he forced himself to do it anyway. He closed his eyes and made himself envision it. It'd have to be a demon that had some kind of symbiotic relationship with humans—or parasitic, rather, whatever gains humans *believed* they got aside—and not one that preyed in any other way. A cubant, maybe. Those didn't want their lovers dead while there was still something to get from them.

He replayed the scene from yesterday, imagining a demon sitting there when he came in, instead of just Bruant with his cat. Some human-like shape with hooves, horns, and a tail.

And he tried, he *tried*, to be fair about it, like Tari was asking. He tried to imagine them seeming to get along. The demon laughing, Bruant happy. Tried to take the image of one of Bruant's normal friends and twist it into demonic shape, then put that abomination next to Bruant. *Bruant's lonely; that's why he's found a cat. He lucked out with that needy beast. What if he'd found a demon instead?*

"I don't know," he said finally, defeated.

"You don't know what you'd do?" Tari asked softly.

"I still feel like I'd run the demon off. Convince Bruant. He'd have to understand." He hesitated, drawn forward despite his insistence. "But if he didn't want to be convinced..."

Tari said, "Would you try to see if the Inquisition could straighten him out? Get rid of that demonic influence?"

"*No*," Pel said, aghast. He was strangely relieved that he hadn't felt the need to hesitate. "He's my *son*."

She was silent a moment longer, watching him with those clear eyes. It looked uncomfortably like she'd realized something from that, but he couldn't figure out what.

"Then, would you let him keep seeing the demon?" Her tone and face were both distantly thoughtful, nothing else, and almost impossible to read.

"I couldn't," Pel said. It came out raw.

"And that's why you don't know. Because what alternatives are there?"

He stared at her. She was motionless beneath him and still, despite the pain that he could taste with each breath, attractive. But the conversation left him cold, even with the physical heat of his reaction.

"Well," she said, and smiled again. "At least it's just a theoretical exercise. But I guess you can see why I didn't think it was funny?"

Almost queasy with horror, he stumbled to his feet. "Yeah," he said. "Sure. I have to—I have to go get ready for opening."

"Sure," she said, but he'd already left her behind him as he made his escape.

~~*

Pel replayed that image over and over again throughout work: Bruant and a demon sitting together, laughing and talking. Himself bursting in. *What would I have done?*

He knew it was impacting his business, if only a little. He had to ask for orders to be repeated, and kept losing his smile as he got distracted by his own thoughts. Even this preoccupied, he couldn't turn off that part of his mind which paid attention to people, and he caught the way his patrons were looking at him. He'd snap his attention back, only to have it wander off again as soon as the conversation changed.

They weren't the only ones noticing his lack of focus. When the day was finally over and everyone else had cleared out, Bruant came downstairs to help and Pel found himself staring at Bruant on the stairs like he'd been a ghost walking down instead.

He saw it all at once: The nightmare image of Bruant dead at a demon's hands, made worse by his similarity to Phalene. The laughing image of Bruant next to some demon he'd horrifically decided to befriend. The real Bruant, standing in front of him.

"Dad?" Bruant froze in place under Pel's gaze like

a spooked animal. He shifted uncomfortably on the last stair before taking it and coming around the bar to face him. "You okay? You look like you saw a ghost."

Pel shook himself out of his distraction. *Get it together, Pel.* "Sorry, Bru," he said weakly. "I'm not really feeling well right now."

"Uh, yeah, you look it." Bruant made a false start, then stepped closer. He pushed the back of his hand to Pel's forehead. "You don't feel warm or anything, but you still look pretty lousy."

Pel smiled at Bruant and hoped it looked reassuring. "I'll be fine," he said. "Just gotta push through. Lots of work to be done."

He picked up his mop and went to fill a bucket from the pump by the sink. When he looked back again, Bruant was worrying his lower lip with his teeth.

Their eyes met. Pel realized he didn't know what expression was on his face anymore, and forced a smile again.

That seemed to decide Bruant. He straightened up, setting his jaw, and held out a hand. "Give me that," he said, gesturing at the mop. "You go to bed."

"I'm fine, Bru," Pel protested. "It's a lot of work. It'll go faster with the two of us."

Despite Pel's objections, Bruant took hold of the mop handle, tugging at it almost too insistently. Holding the bucket with his other hand, Pel was forced to let go after the third yank for fear of spilling the water.

Some of Bruant's anger seemed to be creeping back in again when he looked up, clutching the mop tightly to his chest, breathing hard. This time, though, Pel thought it might be different. Like this guilt, *this* anger, had gone inward.

"You've been worrying a lot lately, huh?" Bruant said.

"I'm fine—"

"Stop *saying* that," Bruant said. He moved to rub the back of his forehead with a fist and almost whacked himself with the mop shaft. "Damn—"

Pel opened his mouth to protest again, then closed it, not sure what to say. He tried again. "You've been worrying a lot, too," he said. "I know it's... hard. What you learned."

"Yeah," Bruant said, looking at the floor as intently as if he planned to find all the dirt by sight before cleaning up. "But we're not talking about me right now."

"I'd rather."

"Of course you'd rather," Bruant muttered, not quite under his breath. He ran a hand down the mop handle like he was grounding himself, and found some of the impatience Pel was more used to from him. "Dad, let *me* say it: It's fine. I can handle this tonight. You go to bed. We can talk again when you've gotten some rest."

"But—"

"You think this conversation's gonna go well when you feel like shit?" Bruant asked, voice rising a little. "'Cause I can see a lot of ways we'd mess that up."

Well, that's fucking hard to disagree with. Pel rubbed the back of his head, searching for protests, and, finding no reasonable ones, gave up. "Well, all right," he said finally. "But just for tonight. I really don't like to leave you alone to clean up in here."

"I'm not alone," Bruant said, with a quick uncertain grin, as if waiting for Pel to start arguing again. He pointed to Kip, who had hopped up on one of the tables and was washing between his splayed toes. "I've at least got company."

The sight made Pel smile involuntarily. He was embarrassed to realize how strange a natural smile felt on his face—he'd gotten too used to forcing them, somewhere down the line.

Bruant was right. He needed rest.

"Fine, fine." Pel sighed. He put the bucket down on the counter and raised both hands, shrugging expansively. "You got me. I'll leave it to you, but you make sure that cat pulls his weight, all right? It's a two-person job."

Bruant let out a laugh, seeming as surprised by the sound as Pel had been by his own smile. *We're a wreck*, Pel thought mournfully.

"Yes, sir," Bruant said, with an incorrectly executed salute.

Pel saluted back, matching the error.

He made his way upstairs, past Bruant's empty room, down the hall further beyond the guest rooms, then paused outside Tari's absolutely *not* empty room. There, in front of the door, he could hear the sounds from inside, and felt himself flush.

For a moment, he was fantasizing about it: Himself in there, instead of whoever she'd drawn in today. Imagining her underneath. Her hair spread out on the pillow, her fingernails on his back, her legs wrapped around him—

Some innkeeper, he thought, flustered, *voyeuring your guests*.

He hurried on back to his room.

But it was hard to keep from thinking about it. She had someone in every night, and clearly was comfortable having sex with just about anyone. But although the two of them seemed to be getting closer, she hadn't propositioned him. As the innkeeper, he reminded himself for what was nowhere near the first time, it would be wrong to make the first move.

He tried to put the thought out of his mind as he slid onto his own bed with a heavy sigh, taking his boots off. But forcing himself not to think of that just made the image of Bruant and a demon rise in his mind again, and he tried to force *that* out too—

The images overlapped. Tari with a demon, drawing some monster on top of her to fuck.

He scrubbed at his face. *Tari with a demon. Gods above, she'd probably eat them alive.*

And then another thought occurred and he froze, boot still in his hand.

She had sex every night. Possibly more, if she looked for it again during the day while she was out. And she wore her partners out. It was reasonable, he reminded himself. It was a normal, human thing to do—some people just really liked to fuck. There was no crime in it.

But he couldn't stop thinking about it now. The other things that hadn't made sense all rose up at once. She didn't want to move on until she'd resupplied, which she needed money to do, but she seemed to have enough money to pay Pel indefinitely. Sure, her explanation had been convincing enough. But she was popular and charismatic; was there really no jeweler in town who'd buy the lot of her gems all at once?

She might not look like a succubus, but that didn't mean anything. Succubi were shapeshifters. They were, in fact, the same thing as incubi and the states in between. Humans had just named them differently in the early days of the demon invasion, assuming an inherent sexual binary with no shapeshifting. That had turned out to be flat-out wrong—they were inclined to fit into a binary even less than humans were. Still, would it even be possible for a cubant to maintain a human shape for this long?

But why wouldn't it be? How much energy might shapeshifting even use?

He knew he was being paranoid again. She was reasonable, thoughtful. Blunt but kind. If she were a demon, why would she come here? Would someone like her really take on a demon-hating city just for the chance to feed where other demons weren't?

Then again, if she were a demon, that would mean he'd never understood her at all.

Pel groaned, dropping his boot and grinding the heels of his hands against his closed eyes until he saw stars. "I'm too tired," he muttered. "I'm stressed out. This isn't making any sense."

But even as he tried to force himself to shake the it off, he found himself feeling more and more sure it might be the truth.

Slowly, he took a few steady breaths, and thought: *And then what?*

If Tari *were* a demon and he'd found it out, what would he do?

The worst she'd done to anyone here was tire them out. She hadn't made a move on Bruant—Pel was still pretty sure Bruant would have given it away if she had. Bruant clearly liked her, but he seemed to do so as a friend or mentor, not a lover. So she wasn't hunting indiscriminately. And the different lovers every night... Even if she were feeding on people, she was at least spreading the damage around instead of focusing on a single target.

Was it possible for a demon to be harmless? Or, at least, to *mean* no harm? Tari had implied that it was, but how trustworthy was anything she'd said about demons if she were one herself?

He didn't know what he'd do.

But *whatever* he'd do about it, he needed to know what she was, one way or another. Avoiding the subject was just plain dangerous.

And he couldn't just ask her. Not and expect an honest answer, at any rate—he was sure he'd get a laugh and then a light, "I'm obviously human," regardless of whether or not it were true.

There was always the amulet.

If it worked on her, she was a demon. But that would be a statement of war, a statement of his intent to harm her and turn her in. She'd definitely react to that, and if she were stronger than the binding, both he and Bruant would be at risk.

There was one other way. The thought occurred, and he groaned again, rubbing his face.

I could seduce her.

He was attracted to her. *Deeply* attracted. If she were a cubant, her demonic powers would have let her know that already. If he made the first move, she'd accept. He was sure of that, especially if she were a succubus. Though that might not mean anything by itself—demon or human, she clearly liked sex.

But if she were a cubant and had sex with him, she'd drain some of his energy. He'd feel it slip away— would try to force himself into awareness—and he could, at that point, use the amulet if he wanted to. What better way to figure out a demon than by seeming to give them exactly what they wanted while paying close attention to whether they took it? To be prepared to act as soon as they tipped their hand? It was a perfect plan.

An awful plan, a terrible thing to do to someone.

But a perfect plan nonetheless.

Chapter Five

Pel had gone to sleep trying to force himself to feel secure in that thought, but as the next day went on, he started to question himself more. He had no intention of changing his plans, but he certainly found himself feeling significantly worse for making them.

Sex under false pretenses was an awful thing to do to someone. It raised issues of morality that he felt fairly certain he'd be on the wrong side of; the other person wouldn't be agreeing to sex with the full knowledge of the terms. Sure, if Tari were a demon, then they'd both be lying to each other. But on some level, it didn't matter what *she* did. One way or another, *his* intentions weren't good.

He wanted to pretend it would be fine. He truly did. He was into her. He liked her. He'd want to do this anyway, just out of hope of something growing between them. If she weren't a demon, he really could trust her.

But if she were, he couldn't. No matter how he thought about it through the day, he couldn't think of a better way to find out than to set up his own trap by seeming to walk into hers.

"Bru."

Bruant glanced over from where he was helping set up for the evening. His cat had jumped onto his shoulder and somehow kept himself perched there, despite how much Bruant was moving around; it gave

Bruant a weird, hunched silhouette. "Dad?"

Pel felt himself begin to flush even before he spoke. "Could I ask you—that is to say, there's a good chance that I might need you to run the bar tonight."

"Sure, if you need me to. I don't have plans. Still feeling sick?" Sudden concern showed on Bruant's face as he looked Pel over.

It was no surprise that Bruant was worried, since Pel usually only asked for help when he was too unwell to manage. He found himself fumbling a tankard, almost dropping it twice before he gave up and just put it down. "There's something I need to talk to Tari about later and—well, you know how busy she gets in the evening—"

"Busy," Bruant repeated, the word a barked laugh, short and fast. "Yeah, I think everyone knows that."

"Yes," Pel said, strained. "Well, I'd like to talk to her tonight, and it might take a while, so—"

It only took a moment for realization to dawn, leaving Bruant looking half smug and half horrified, face screwing up. A reasonable response, Pel thought with embarrassment, to any boy's realization that his father might be looking to get laid.

"*So*," Pel said, a little too loudly, "I think it would be best if you mind things. Here. Tonight. It'll be good training for you."

"I already said yes!" Bruant protested, voice rising in what was nearly a yelp. Kip shifted from his right shoulder to his left, rubbing against the back of his head as if trying to soothe him. "Look, I'm glad to see you finally interested in someone again, but don't tell me any more about it!"

"I just—yes. No. I won't," Pel muttered, and rubbed his face with both hands.

"Just... just finish helping me get things set up, all right?"

Pel shook himself. "Of course," he said, then cut himself off, head jerking up as the door opened; beside him, Bruant did likewise.

He stared at Tari as she shut the door behind herself, and was peripherally aware of Bruant doing the same. Turning to see them, her eyebrows slowly raised. "Uh, yes?" she said. "Something on my face? I didn't forget my pants anywhere, right?" She looked down, lifting first one leg, then the other, in a mock-examination.

"No," Pel said, then flushed. He was obviously being teased. He cleared his throat. "Uh, do you have a moment?"

"I surely do," she said slowly. "Do you? You're normally getting ready for work right now, aren't you?"

He tried to find something to say. It'd all fall apart right now if he kept floundering, but he couldn't seem to find the right kind of words to invite her upstairs, failing to find the balance between too blunt and too vague. Trying to charm people was one thing, but trying to flirt, actively moving toward a genuine attempt to go somewhere with it—*Gods, but it's been too many long years.*

Too cheerily to pass for normal, Bruant said, "Dad thinks I should try to run the bar alone tonight to see how I'll handle it! So I'll be taking over for him today."

"Is that so?" Tari came over, stretching, then ruffled Bruant's hair. "Good luck, kiddo. Don't let the Villem boys eat you alive out there."

Bruant ducked under it, making a face. "It's not the first time or anything, but thanks. It'll be fine."

"I didn't say it wouldn't be fine," Tari said, voice teasing. "I said *good luck*."

Pel, watching them, found his breath had decided to take his leave without permission. A mess of emotions welled up in him: guilt at what he was about to do, anger at himself and the situation, hope that maybe she was human after all. She fit so nicely in their family, teasing Bruant like she'd known him for years.

Even as he thought it, though, he chided himself more. It wasn't right to cast her in that role, especially without her permission. She didn't seem like someone who could be pinned down to one person, or who would want to stay in one place.

And she was, perhaps, too much like Phalene, who had wanted something more than what she'd had, wanted adventure and travel and to experience what this city didn't allow, and it had killed her. He didn't think he could handle that a second time.

Besides, under the circumstances, it wasn't something he dared consider. Absurd to be trying to entrap her and to find himself longing to be wrong at the same time.

He was startled out of his thoughts as Kip, apparently having enough with the roughhousing as Tari got Bruant into a headlock, leaped off Bruant and landed on Pel. He froze at the sudden shifting weight, worried that the cat might slip and claw him, but Kip just headbutted him gently in the jaw before staring at him from far too close.

Tari laughed. "Looks like he likes you," she commented.

And that was damn weird. Pel had barely interacted with the animal, following Tari's advice in leaving him to be something for his son, rather than something they shared. And Kip had seemed uninterested in anyone but Bruant.

But even so, gazing into the animal's gold eyes, he found himself relaxing, the frustration and anger melting away. It was abruptly easy to see why someone as emotional as Bruant would be so comforted to have the creature around.

"Hup, let me get him off you," Tari said, putting her hands around the cat's ribs and lifting him off Pel. Kip let out a protesting meow but settled down at once as she handed him back to Bruant. "You looked like you were afraid to move, Pel."

"A little bit," Pel admitted. He drew a deep breath and let it out slowly, then took advantage of the current mood to hold out a hand to her.

She blinked, then smiled at him a little coyly as she took it. "What's this about?"

"I asked if you had a moment," he reminded her.

"And I said I did. Several moments, really," she added. "Maybe more."

"Will you come upstairs with me?" he asked.

Tari only looked at him, eyes calm and measuring. Then she folded her hand more tightly with his, sliding their fingers together, and led the way to the stairs.

Shit. I promised to help Bru with the setup.

Well, whatever. Bruant could manage it.

Tari stopped at the door to her room, but he shook his head, tugging on their joined hands, leading her to his room instead. It was half to comfort himself—both in terms of the familiarity and to know he had his amulet in the drawer next to the bed, where he'd stored it ages ago for easy grabbing if something happened in the night—and half to keep her off kilter, away from whatever protections she might have set up on her own room.

If she *were* a demon, anyway.

Tari went willingly enough, hand tightening on his more in what seemed like reassurance to him than any alarm of her own. He let her in, dropped her hand, and walked over to the bed. "I—"

He turned, and was surprised to see she'd followed him immediately and was standing close, well within his personal bubble. She grinned at him, amused. "You wanted to talk?"

"I didn't say that I wanted to *talk*," he said, and immediately winced. That hadn't been suave at all. Demanding, maybe, which he didn't think was terribly attractive. "I—"

Tari watched him, head tilted, that amused expression still on her face. And then it shifted somehow into something softer, even a touch wistful. "Are you sure?"

Pel blinked, and drew an unsteady breath. His self-doubts welled up again like water from a wrung cloth. *Redirect them. Disguise them.* "I'm sorry. I'm doing this all wrong."

"Little bit," she said, fondly teasing. "But I just meant that you look troubled. Do you want to tell me about it? Maybe I can make you feel better."

"No," he said. It came out hoarse. "I don't."

"Then, do you want to distract yourself?" she asked, and reached out, sliding a hand against his jaw, brushing the scars there.

He felt terrible. But even so, her touch was warm and appealing. She smelled good, he noticed, from this close.

It didn't feel terrible to want her, at least. Just to

know why he was acting on it.

"Yeah," he breathed.

"All right," she said comfortably, and leaned in.

She kissed on the knife's edge of sweetness and promise, a hint of teeth and tongue in between gentle movements. He drew a sharp breath in through his nose and kissed her back clumsily, long out of practice, wrapping his arms around her and feeling her narrow frame against his body.

Pel heard himself make a sound, wanting her helplessly, and, momentarily, he let himself give in to desire. He *did* want to distract himself, to forget his suspicions and fears and anger and his old, old memories that wouldn't go away. To feel her and enjoy her and have her enjoy him. To make her feel good. He wanted, after, to lie with her and laugh together. He wanted to think of a future, and, fuck, that was a lot of pressure to put on himself, let alone another person, but he wanted, he *wanted*—

Tari drew Pel down onto the bed and sat with him, thigh pressed to thigh as they twisted to kiss each other. He tangled his fingers in her thick hair, her perfect, never-tangled hair, and held her in place as he kissed her roughly. She pressed both hands to his jaw, uncalloused fingers catching at his ears and the fine hairs at the back of his neck, rubbing there.

It was good. More *than good*. Every touch of her fingers seemed to burn their way into him. It had been too long, he thought as he slid his hand from her hair down her neck, resting on her shoulder. Too much time spent with grief forming a wall between him and anyone else. Too many years of ghosts and memories welling up under his fingertips when he'd tried to press them to anyone else.

He groaned, tilting his head back as she mouthed along his neck, feeling her grin a little.

"You're so sensitive," she breathed.

"It's been... a while," he said, not sure exactly why he was admitting it except for how intrusive the thought was.

"That's all right," she murmured, eyes heavy. "Don't worry about anything."

She unfastened the laces of his shirt before pulling back enough to help tug it over his head. He leaned forward to make that easier for her, and drew a deep breath when it came off, as though it had been restricting him somehow.

Tari looked at him with heated eyes, grinning a little and biting down on her lower lip. "Well, damn," she said. "Don't you look good."

Pel flushed a little, self-conscious, but smiled back. He wasn't as fit as he was in his youth, but he was, at the moment, extremely relieved he still exercised. He reached for her again, putting both hands on her waist as Tari ran a hand over his chest, fingers combing through the hair in the center briefly on their way outward, until she found a nipple and traced a fingernail over it.

The shock of pleasure that it sent through him was surprisingly sharp, and he groaned, feeling his hard cock twitch in his pants. "Damn. Tari..."

"Mmhm?"

"Let me..." He leaned forward to do the same to her, unbuttoning her shirt, exposing warm brown skin in a slowly growing strip toward her navel, then pushed it off her shoulders, showing small, firm breasts with pointed dark nipples.

Pel's breath caught. He wanted her so badly.

But this is wrong.

He couldn't do this. Whether she were a human or a demon, he was taking advantage of her to try to trap her. Even if she turned out to be human, it didn't change what he was doing. He had thought he would be capable of that—he'd thought it was justifiable. Finding a line he couldn't cross was a surprise.

But a line was a line.

Pel's gaze jerked up to her face, and he saw caution there. She'd seen him hesitate, and she was responding to it with more care than an innocent would necessarily have.

He had to find out one way or another. It was a stupid idea. He'd already decided that. But even so, he heard himself blurt it out:

"You're not human," he asked, hearing it come out plaintive. Stupid. Begging for honesty, and knowing she'd lie if she were dishonest. "Are you?"

She sighed. Unselfconscious in her near nudity but unhappy now, she lifted a hand and pushed some of her hair back.

"No," she said, tone heavy. "Sorry. Uh, can we still do this?"

He could do nothing but stare at her. She looked unrepentant about it—matter-of-fact, really, gazing back at him with more resignation than guilt.

His next inhalation seemed to burn his lungs as rage welled up.

Pel grabbed Tari's wrist with his right hand at the same time as he grabbed his bedside drawer with his left, yanking it open so hard that it almost went flying. He'd cleared out all but one thing, however, making it easy to grab the string of the amulet in his fist.

Tari let out a groan of displeasure as he did so but

didn't pull away even as he thrust the binding amulet in her face. She didn't flinch or show any other visible reaction to it.

"Tell me, demon," he said, and wished his voice wasn't shaking—wished, if he couldn't stop it, that it sounded as though he was shaking with rage instead of betrayal. "What's your true name? You're no Toutarelle."

"Still Tari," Tari said, voice finally a little strained. "Tarigan. You don't need to try to control me, sweetheart, I answered when you asked me properly."

"Tarigan. By your name, I demand you answer my questions."

Judging from her actual flinch, *that* little bit of demonology he'd picked up from the Inquisition seemed to be true: a demon was bound by their name more than by any object. Mixed with the amulet's warding, it should force her to obey.

"Pel, *please*," Tari said, more strained than before, but with an exaggerated patience, somehow putting sarcasm into every word. "*I'm answering them*, sweetheart."

He didn't want to hear her call him by the nickname she'd given him. He shook the amulet, half to cover his trembling. He needed to keep his momentum up or he wasn't sure he could do this. Not again. "What kind of demon are you?"

"Cubant," Tari said, strained and forcing a smile. "Though I think you figured that out already. You're holding my wrist a bit tight."

He fought the urge to loosen his grip. "You gave yourself away."

"Yeah, I realized," Tari said. "Probably in a lot of ways. Somehow I got comfortable around you. I usually default between sexes, and since it didn't look like you were going to go for me and find out, I let myself just look how I usually do for a few days there."

"Between—?" Pel found himself fumbling the conversation.

"Between. I'm usually a they, not a he or a she. I enjoy it most when I'm an intercubus, not an incubus or succubus. I was a bit concerned that correcting your immediate assumption could have given me away even faster in a suspicious place like this," Tari said dryly, "so I let you think I was female. Once sex was on the table, I thought I'd change to keep up with the assumption."

With a sudden squirm against Pel's grip on their wrist, Tari's body shifted just slightly, as though they were exhaling a breath they'd been holding, making their small breasts smaller, wide shoulders wider. A more familiar figure, even when Pel hadn't noticed that the one he'd been touching was unfamiliar at all, too caught up in touching *Tari* to notice anything else.

Pel shook his head, trying to clear his blush away, trying to focus again. "That's not the point," he said. "I don't—care about that. That doesn't have anything to do with anything—" Why had they even brought it up? Trying to distract him?

Tari blinked. "Wait, you didn't notice I'd shapeshifted? I thought that was why you asked."

He stared at Tari, forcing himself to keep his gaze on their face.

"You really didn't. Man," Tari groused, "I was sure it'd be that and now I'm all embarrassed. So I guess it was something else that clued you in. So what was it? My personality? A little too worldly for a human lifespan, was that it?"

She's still so herself. Themself. "Shut *up*, demon."

"You *just* got my name—"

Pel was rapidly losing control of the situation, and knew it. He shook Tari's wrist, yanking them forward. The amulet was pressing against their cheek now, and they made an expression like they could smell something unpleasant.

"Tell me, Tarigan," he said, as coldly as he could manage, "why did you come here? What do you want from us? From myself, from Bruant, from this city?"

Tari tilted their head back, a muscle in their jaw jumping. It seemed more like annoyance than tension. "Put that thing down, okay? I'll answer honestly, Pel. I owe you that for all the help you've given me here—"

He didn't put the amulet down. "*Tell me.*"

Tari sighed. Their arm tensed like they were planning to use demonic strength to pull away despite the presence of the binding amulet—and then they just relaxed instead, sagging back into the bed.

He found himself leaning over them again in order to keep the amulet in their face. Tari's wrist was over their head, still in his grip, but they seemed to be doing their best to get comfortable regardless, tucking their other hand behind their head as a makeshift pillow, closing their eyes.

Despite everything he knew now, it was still erotic to see them lying on the bed like that, half-naked and practically beneath him. That sense of betrayal welled up in him again, and he gritted his teeth, about to repeat his question.

Tari started speaking before he had the chance. "I'm not here to hurt anyone, Pel. I know you probably won't believe me, especially with what you've gone through, but I'm not." They opened their eyes slowly, looking up at him again. "Are you willing to believe me, or at least, try to?"

It was exactly what he wanted to hear, and he couldn't help but wonder if they knew that. He bit his lower lip almost too hard and then shrugged once. "Go on," he said.

A smile passed over Tari's lips briefly. It didn't stay, vanishing like it was on a trip and had only needed a place to rest. "Look, sweetheart, I'm not young," they said finally. "So I get bored. And I'm not old, so I don't get set in my ways. I like people. I like exploring new things. I wanted to see what it was like in a city like this. As you'd guessed, we do get curious about the places we're not allowed to go."

"How did you fool the guards?" He refused to let himself get sidetracked.

Tari shrugged. "I just answered their questions. When they bled me, I made blood. Shapeshifters have an easier time than some demons, and cubants have the easiest time of all. We're very familiar with humanity."

Getting more frustrated, he pushed harder. "How did you get around their wards?"

"Trade secret."

"*Tarigan.*"

"That *is* my name," they agreed, annoyed. Then, "Honestly, it's just a cubant thing, because we're so physical. We still feel wards and they affect us, but they do so *less* than more spirit-like demons. It's not comfortable but it's easier. We're weak in other areas to compensate, mind, but even what you're doing now, I could make myself not answer—at least for a little while. I can't get up and go anywhere while you're doing that, but I'm *choosing* to talk to you, Pel."

That explained the amount of back-talk, at least. Pel slowly lowered his hand a little, cautious that they might be lying. But then, if Tari could break the binding enough to lie, they had to be telling the truth—

"I just wanted to know what it was like. I've never seen humans without demons around before," Tari said, a little wistful. "And I like... I *like* humans. Though I mostly like teaching humans about demons, so that's not an option here. But I thought it'd be educational, to see that... lack. That emptiness. The space where demons aren't."

Pel made himself breathe slowly and gently around the ache that soft tone brought up. "And what do you think now that you have?"

"Looks to me like you've compensated for the lack of demons by becoming predators all on your own," Tari said seriously, a faint line of concern between their brows. "Maybe you always were, even before we came to your world. Not sure how I feel about that. Really not sure. At least some of you are still cute and willing to compromise. Your son has the right idea."

That was the wrong thing to say. There was a moment where Pel thought that, calm, before the anger hit again, like water drawn back from the shore before a crushing wave came down.

It smashed into him. He grabbed their wrist harder and slammed it down to the bed, leaning over them, resting the amulet against their face again. They flinched, then looked up at him with no other reaction, unsmiling.

"What the hell is that supposed to mean, Tarigan?" he demanded. "*What have you done to Bruant?*"

Tari sighed heavily. "All I meant," they said, in a tone like this all was more an imposition than a threat, "was that it's good to see someone like Bruant *questioning* your way of life. Frankly, I think everyone should. Question what it's like to live under demons. Question what it's like not to. Question what it means to live alongside them, what they are, how to face them with confidence."

"Answer *my* question," he growled. "What have you done to Bruant? Have you slept with him? Have you hurt him, have you—"

"That's a good question!" Tari said in an irritably cheery tone. "The answer is no—no to all of it—but you have no reason to believe me, and if you don't believe me, you believe he's under demonic influence. But, more to the point, say you use your binding here and my name to try to turn me over to the Inquisition, wear me down with it until I have to go along. If I tell *them* that I've influenced Bruant, that he's mine now—whether he is or not, what will happen to him?"

Pel stared at them, mind going blank with shock.

"I'm just wondering what my options are here," Tari said evenly, "given that you've told me you don't know what you'd do to a demon you caught."

How had I let myself like this person, this demon? How had he let himself become so weak to someone he already suspected?

There was only one option. Only one way to protect Bruant. The same answer he'd come to in an earlier discussion with Tari.

"Get out," he hissed.

Their eyes widened. "What—?"

"Get out. I won't tell the Inquisition anything," he said. His throat ached, like the words were clawing it up as they came out. "And in return, you don't breathe a word about my son to anyone. I don't hurt you, you don't hurt us. Fine?"

Tari's brows drew down. "Pel, calm down. Honestly, I haven't done anything to Bru and I don't want to. I just don't like being threatened. Look, I'm not going to—"

"Get out," he said louder. "Take your stuff. Find a new place to stay. I won't say anything about you, I won't hamper you in doing whatever you *really* want to do here. You just leave my family alone."

Slowly, still holding the amulet tightly in case the decision gave Tari an opening to attack, he let go of their wrist and sat back. Tari lay on his bed a moment longer, breathing hard, then pushed their palms against the bed, shuffling backward, away from him.

They finally seemed visibly upset, face tight, brows still twisted. "Honestly, Pel. I wasn't going to do anything. I like—"

He didn't wait to hear the end of that, didn't wait to hear if it was his own name or Bruant's or *humans* or something worse. "Get out! I won't give you access to my son any more. The rest of the city can be damned, but you need to *leave!*"

Tari rolled to the side, hauling themself off the bed, dragging their shirt with them. They kept their hands raised, one palm out, shirt hanging from the other in a fist, as if indicating they were unarmed. As though that meant anything to a demon. "Okay. I'm going, Pel. I'm—sorry."

He felt, for a moment, that they meant it—which made it even worse.

Shaking off that thought, he followed them to the door, breathing hard, his throat tight. "And if you try anything against Bruant," he said, a hoarse whisper, "if you hurt him—I'll tell the Inquisition everything. Even if they drag me down, too, I won't give a damn so long as I get my revenge. You understand?"

"I understand," Tari said coolly. "I'm getting my things and leaving now."

"Go," he said.

He didn't follow them any further, just waited until he heard Tari's door further down the hall open before he stumbled back a few steps to sit on his bed.

It was done. The demon was leaving.

His family was free.

~~*

He was still there several hours later—though now lying on his back, gazing up at the ceiling and barely keeping his head above the poisonous cloud of his thoughts—when the bar closed for the night and Bruant rapped on the door.

"Dad?" His voice was muffled, tone indistinct.

Pel hadn't locked the door since sending Tari out of it. "Come in."

He heard the door handle turn. Pel didn't sit up or look over, just saw Bruant approach in his peripheral vision, stopping at the side of the bed.

Something landed on the pillow next to him, then slid off. He turned his head.

A room key.

Tari's room key.

"Tari left in a hurry earlier," Bruant said, accusatory. "She was carrying all her stuff. She gave me her key back and said she had to go."

"Mm," Pel said.

"What did you do to her?" Bruant asked, voice tight with a restrained anger.

Pel groaned. He rubbed hard at his forehead with the heel of his hand, as though he could somehow shove away the thoughts and feelings through physical effort alone. "I did what I had to do."

"Bullshit," Bruant said, and kicked the side of the bed with a thump.

That finally forced Pel to look at him, sighing as he sat up, running fingers through his hair. *I'm too tired for this.* "Did Tari do anything to *you*?"

"She ruffled my hair and said 'I'll miss you, kiddo'." Bruant spat it venomously, but he looked more hurt than angry.

Pel forced himself to not close his eyes again despite the jab of pain. "No. Before that. Did you sleep together?"

Bruant choked. "Uh, I wouldn't have encouraged you to go after her if we had!"

He'd thought not. He'd *hoped* not. But you never knew with demons how they might twist you around what they wanted, how they might convince you to shrug off your concerns. "Good," he said, sighing. "Bruant, she—they—Tari's a demon."

"So?" Bruant said. His eyes were strained, braced for confrontation, and he set his jaw in a way that reminded Pel so much of Phalene that she could have been standing there in his place.

He braced himself for a hard fight. Phalene had been one of the most stubborn people he'd ever met.

"What do you mean, *so*?" Pel protested. "They're dangerous. Tari's been using this inn as a base of operations since they got here. Taking people to bed every night and feeding on them—"

Bruant scoffed aloud, gesturing wildly with one hand. "It's not like Tari *hurt* them! I'm pretty sure anyone who got with Tari would kinda enjoy it! So who cares? Everyone has to eat—"

Pel drew in a sudden shocked breath of realization. "You aren't surprised."

"Dad..."

"You knew." Pel clenched his hands on the bed, trying to keep himself from getting up. Their proximity, his height, would guarantee he'd loom over Bruant, and as angry as he was, he didn't want to turn this into an intimidation match. "You knew Tari was a demon."

And you didn't warn me. Not even when you knew I was pursuing them.

Bruant flung his hands up, too frustrated to stay still, his long fingers crooked into claws with tension. "Yeah, I knew! They told me!"

"They *told* you?" Pel asked, almost more stunned than angry. "When? How? And you didn't tell me?!"

"Why would I tell *you*?" Bruant fired back. "You made it perfectly clear to me about what you'd do with demons or people who consort with them. But you know what I think?"

Exhaustion was coming in waves again between the pulses of anger, dragging Pel around like snow in a storm. "What do you think, Bru?" he asked, doing his best to keep his voice even.

"I think Tari's a good demon," Bruant said, voice rising. "Tari was *fine*. What does it *matter* if they're a demon? I know how you feel about them, and yeah, Mom died. Some demons are awful. And they all feed on humans, but why is that... why are you so sure it's always just that? Can't it be something both parties get something from? Can't it be some kind of give and take? Tari liked to laugh and help me and just *enjoy* things." His tone had turned pleading. "How's that so bad? Can't we find a balance?"

Could they have? Tari had thought so, or, at least, had *said* so. But—

"Tari *threatened you*, Bru!" he yelled, hands tight on the edge of the mattress to keep himself from moving, to keep Bruant the one over him rather than the other way around. "When I confronted them, Tari threatened to turn you over to the Inquisition to keep themselves safe! Does that sound like someone you can trust? Someone fine, someone *good*?"

Bruant recoiled, wild-eyed. "What? No—you're lying," he said. And then, because he knew, even upset, that Pel wouldn't lie to him about this, "You probably made them!"

That was it. Pel rose. "Get out of my room, Bru!" he bellowed. "You can laugh it off, but I can't. I love you! You're my *son*. I didn't do anything to them—I let them go, I let them leave, because if I didn't—" He cut himself off. There was no point in being cruel and going into the details of Tari's threats on Bruant. "Just lay *off* and—and go to your room!"

Bruant went pale, though with anger rather than fear. It looked like he was going to scream something back, and Pel prepared himself for some kind of verbal jab, something terrible he'd never unhear.

But Bruant just said, "*Fine*," and stomped out, slamming Pel's door behind him.

Pel listened, concerned when he didn't hear an echoing slam from Bruant's room. But there was no way he could follow Bruant now to see if his anger had switched to despair. No way to try to make things right.

He just sat heavily on the bed and buried his face in his hands again as tears welled up.

Chapter Six

Pel didn't get much sleep that night, and what little he got was awful. To make matters worse, when he came down late the next morning, he found—unsurprisingly—that none of the cleanup from the night before had been done.

That's fair, he decided, staring at the mess in exhaustion. Bruant had come to talk as soon as work ended, and then Pel had told him to go to his room. There wasn't exactly a chance for Bruant to have gotten to it even if he'd wanted.

He considered, briefly, going up to Bru's room and calling him down to clean. Maybe they could talk more while they worked together—

But what more was there to say? They both had their opinions on how things should go, and neither could meet in the middle. So he did the cleaning himself, spending a few hours mopping and sweeping and putting things away as morning turned into afternoon.

When he was done, Bruant still hadn't come down. Was he just staying up there to spite Pel at this point? Like he wouldn't come out until Pel gave him permission? Pel scrubbed his hand over his face. He *did* need to talk to Bruant, if only to apologize for yelling. He knew that. *I'll tell him we have to agree to disagree.* Bruant should at least understand that he did it out of love, not hate. Surely that would matter.

Not wanting to give himself time to change his mind, Pel went up to Bruant's room, but he found it empty. In fact, it looked like Bruant hadn't slept there—though he couldn't be sure, not with how rarely Bruant actually made his bed. The cat wasn't there either, and the window was closed.

It disturbed him to think that perhaps Bruant hadn't gone back to his room at all. Had he gone right out and tried to track Tari down? Hopefully not. If he *had* tried, hopefully he hadn't succeeded.

Perhaps, Pel thought tiredly, he just had gone to stay with a friend, get some space between them so he could cool down.

It wouldn't be the first time that had happened, even before all this.

After dithering around a little longer, Pel gave up on being productive and made himself lunch. Wanting to be at home just in case Bruant came back, he skipped his pre-meal workout, substituting it by mixing himself a strong drink to wash it down with. *Little early to start*, he thought with grim humor, *but it feels like the occasion calls for it.*

He was mid-meal and on his second drink when Bruant finally walked in, slow and exhausted-looking, cat winding between his feet as he walked.

Pel finished chewing his bite and put his meat bun back down on the plate. "Bru," he said, rough.

Bruant jumped; he apparently hadn't seen Pel there until he spoke. "Father," he said finally.

Whether he'd cooled his head or was simply too tired to be angry, Bruant seemed much more subdued, the circles under his eyes both dark and ashen. Kip, apparently anxious from hearing the yelling the night before, sat behind Bruant's legs and peeked out around them, ears pinned.

"Where did you go?" Pel asked evenly.

"Just out," Bruant said, and looked away from him. "Went for a walk. Stayed out with a friend. I didn't go try to find Tari, if that's what you're thinking."

"Mm," Pel said, noncommittally. Bruant was obviously lying about *some* part of that, if not all of it. "I'm sorry I yelled at you."

Bruant scrubbed both hands through his hair, leaving it more of a mess than before. "Yeah, well. Nothing to do about it now. You've made your choice."

"I'm not happy about it either," Pel said.

After a moment of just watching him with sunken eyes, Bruant shrugged. "This isn't really about being happy. Not for you. I get that. But maybe you can consider *my* happiness sometime."

To keep himself from saying the wrong thing by speaking too soon, Pel picked up his bun and took a bite. He forced himself to chew and swallow it before continuing. "Well. Maybe not where it involves demons. I've got to think of what's best for you."

A fight seemed to hang in the air between them. He could see Bruant starting to wind up for it, that anger pouring through him in the narrowing of his eyes and the hunching of his shoulders—and then vanishing. Bruant crouched, petting Kip a few times and avoiding Pel's eyes. "I've got to think of what's best for me too," Bruant said dully, scooping Kip into his arms. "I'm going to go sleep. I'm tired. Wake me up when it's time to set up tonight."

Something in Pel, something that had been tense since that morning, relaxed.

"I'll do that," he said.

Over the next half-week, they fell into an odd routine. Bruant used to wake up as early as he could and go out, denying himself sleep with the youthful ability to run off food and determination alone. Now, he slept through most of the day, getting up in the afternoon and helping Pel prepare the inn. After dinner, he would head out for a while with Kip padding along after him, both of them returning in time for Bruant to help with closing. After they'd finished cleaning, Bru would usually head back out.

Pel desperately wanted to know where he was going at night and, with equal desperation, didn't dare ask. *It's fine. He threw his sleep schedule off, is frustrated, doesn't want to stay at home with me. At least he's still helping out—he still cares.*

But Pel worried. He worried about what was going on, if Bruant was chasing after Tari, and he worried too about what people might think if they saw Bruant acting strangely. But he didn't dare follow him either. If he did and Bruant found out, it really would wreck what faith remained between them. It was impossible to trust him when he was this afraid, but he had no choice.

He didn't ask for details, either, afraid of how much worse it could get if Bruant felt put on the spot—but avoidance didn't help his mood. He exercised, climbing and sparring and running, all his usual techniques to distract himself, but with no success. He even balanced the bar's ledgers and still wasn't able to stop thinking about Bruant.

At night he sat on the roof and looked at the stars and felt no comfort at all about knowing the rooms beneath him were empty.

Bruant was a man now, Pel told himself. He could manage his own affairs, and the least Pel could do was to try to respect it.

So he tried to focus on his own business. The inn—and the demon who'd stayed there.

It was easy enough to get information on Tari's whereabouts—there was already enough gossip about why he might have kicked Tari out that people were basically updating him without being asked, hoping to learn something interesting in return. Pel kept his own answers to others' questions vague. A disagreement, he told them, but nothing else. It was simply more comfortable for Tari to be elsewhere.

He didn't specify whom it was more comfortable for.

Pel had hoped Tari would leave the city, but it seemed he had no such luck. They had settled in with one of his rivals for housing, Orphie, a widower who rented rooms in a tenement building.

Just as well, Pel thought, a bit vindictively. The walls in Orphie's place were thin and Orphie was strict with her renters, out of determination to not end up accidentally running a whorehouse. In other words, prey would be less available for Tari than it had been in a rowdy pub, and if Tari fed, they would have to do so elsewhere.

The town would, he was sure, be a lot less interesting to Tari when it was starving them.

And so things continued, too soon yet to be considered a habit, while Pel waited for them to change and hoped he wouldn't have to be the one to change it.

A frantic knocking came at the door one evening later that week, as he wiped down glasses and waited for Bruant to return to help set up for the night.

His first thought was that Bruant had forgotten his key—it wouldn't be the first time, and probably wouldn't be the last. But the knocking was too urgent. Concerned, he went over and opened the door, trying to ignore the sinking feeling in the pit of his stomach.

"Yes—?"

He'd barely gotten the word out before he was almost bowled over by someone he'd never seen before in his life.

The young man shoved Pel inside and kicked the door shut behind him, his fists tight in Pel's shirt. Pel staggered under the sudden weight, then snapped his arms up, grabbing the other's wrists and slamming them downward and apart to break the grip.

His immediate panicked assumption was that someone was trying to rob him, but no sooner had he broken the intruder's grip than he realized he was wrong—the boy, no older than Bruant himself, was shaking, sobbing and wailing with great heaving breaths.

Pel stared blankly at him, still gripping his wrists. *Maybe he was robbed and came to the nearest friendly place to get away?* "Are... are you all right?"

The young man sobbed harder, nearly incoherent with it. "Bru—Bru—"

An icy chill ran down Pel's spine. He led the unresisting stranger by the wrists to a stool and sat him down at it, pumping him a glass of water and pressing it into his grip. He had to wrap the young man's shaking fingers around it to force him to hold it securely before he could let go. "What is it? What's happened to Bru? Drink first. Take a deep breath." One of them had to remain calm.

The boy folded his hands around the cup and raised it. Trembling made him a sloppy drinker, water trickling down his chin and darkening the already-dark front of his shirt. He lapped at it with his tongue, tried to take a deep breath, and let out a wet, warbling sound as he sniffled and almost choked on his next sip.

What a weird kid, Pel thought, both his impatience and fear growing as he waited for the young man to finish gulping his water. He looked him over in the meantime. Even though the young man was around Bru's age, he appeared smaller and even more delicate, with a pretty and angular face. He had a puff of short black hair, thick and soft-seeming, and charcoal black skin. Between that and his solid black clothes, he must have blended into the night entirely out there.

Except for his eyes. A rich gold, inhuman and absolutely familiar, they caught the light oddly, gleaming—and it didn't look like it was because of the tears. *I've let a demon into my home*, Pel realized, shocked. Or at least, if not a demon himself, he was someone so demon-touched to visibly show it.

But demon or demon-touched, he had some news about his son. And so he waited, silent, willing himself to ignore his steadily rising sense of dread.

Finally, after what seemed like ages but could only have been a few minutes, the youth sucked a breath in, finding his voice, and said, "Bru got captured. By the guard."

That chill down Pel's spine was pure ice now.

"*Captured?* What do you mean?"

"We were out. I was teaching him. I work best in the moonlight. He got caught. I'm so sorry," the youth blurted. "I'm so sorry! I didn't want anything to happen to him! Since you know the Inquisition, can't you do something? You have to save him! You said you'd do anything to protect him, so please—!"

Shock and anger and terror and grief. They rushed through Pel so hard that he couldn't speak, the air knocked out of him from the sheer force of his emotions. All he could do was stare blankly at the boy—the *demon*—seated hunched over on the stool, trembling so hard that the empty glass was slipping precariously from his weak grip.

Slowly, Pel reached over and took the glass from him, voice low and surprisingly steady. "And you just left him, Kip? You let him get captured?"

Kip's eyes widened, and he burst out with another wail, crouching forward on his seat and pressing his hands to his face as though he could somehow hold the tears in that way. "I had to! I had to! If he's being accused of consorting and had a familiar *right there*, I'd be all the proof they need!"

Pel opened his mouth to respond—to yell, to plead, he didn't know—but was interrupted by another sudden knock at the door, loud and commanding. He froze, paralyzed only for a brief moment before making up his mind and pointing to Kip.

"Behind the counter. *Now.*"

Kip stared at him, eyes wide and luminous, then obediently leapt up, slamming a hand onto the counter top and vaulting it with unnatural grace. Pel didn't bother to take the time to see if Kip got himself hidden—he would, he had to—and headed quickly to the door.

He hadn't locked it behind Kip.

Sure enough, the door opened barely a second later. Roselin, a lieutenant in the Inquisition, took a step inside. "Mr. Stone?"

"What is it?" he demanded. Shaking, he stepped forward. "Did something happen? Bruant was supposed to be home by now!"

Roselin took off her helmet and held it between her hands, expression cool and unreadable despite how many years they'd known each other. "Sir, Bruant Stone has been taken in for colluding with demons."

"What?!" He might have been playing up his confusion, but his anger and horror and fear was all genuine. *Give her what she wants.* He let it seep into his tone, didn't try to disguise it in any way. "Bruant would never. His mother—you *know* what happened to his mother!"

"Yes, sir," Roselin said. She looked at Pel with a stony gaze. "Then you claim you know nothing of his transgressions?"

"I know he didn't *have* any!" Pel said. "Don't fuck with me, Roselin, I've been working for you all this time for *this* bullshit? I promise, if Bruant was up to anything, I'd know about it! You tell them to let my son go!"

She sighed. "Pelerin, I'm letting you know as a courtesy," she said. *Fucking hell she is*, he thought viciously. She was seeing if he was in on it, too. "Your son will be questioned. If he's found innocent, he'll be let go."

"Roselin," he growled, "I've done this for fifteen years and I've never once seen anyone *let go.*"

"You know what's supposed to happen," she said. "They get released outside the city. We'll inform you if that's the case and you can go to him if you wish."

"I've never heard of that happening either," he said.

"Then I hope your son is the first you hear of." She put her helmet back on. "I've known you long enough to believe that you didn't know what he was doing, so I'm glad for that one damn thing, at least. I'm not enjoying this, but your son will not be released until the investigation is complete. I'll try to make it fast. If you discover any further information at home, turn it in at the earliest juncture so we can be done with this as soon as possible. Good evening, Mr. Stone."

She left. Pel stared at the closed door for a long moment, then kicked it hard.

"Ah..."

He startled, then spun, staring at the counter. Kip was peering up from behind it, just the top of his head and his eyes showing.

It's this demon's fault. His damn fault. Pel wondered furiously what the cat fed on, what part of his son he ate, what he got out of this experience, why he'd picked Bruant, of all people.

But still—right now, Kip was the only source of information he had.

He breathed slowly, evenly. "Come out."

"You're so angry at me." Kip almost sounded awed. "But I'm sorry?"

Rage flared, hot. He swallowed it down again, forcibly. Bruant had to come first. "Come out from there, please. I'm not going to hurt you."

Slowly, a pair of hands appeared on the counter top as well. Then Kip pushed himself up, crawling over the counter to sit on the edge of it, his feet on a stool, fingers bunched in the fabric over his knees, facing Pel like one might face one's executioner.

The demon looked—well, miserable. His eyes were swollen with crying, more a burnished brass than gold right now. His face was tight, and he was still trembling terribly hard, apparently in some kind of shock.

Pel closed his eyes, counted to five, and opened them again. "Tari set the Inquisition on you two."

"What...?" Kip blinked, then shook his head furiously. "No! There's no way. They wouldn't do that, I'm sure of it."

"How sure?" Pel said, trying to keep his voice even instead of sinking into a growl. "How well do you know them? Have you two been working together?"

"No, I mean, I met them here," Kip blurted, so desperate it was probably true. He worried at his lower lip with his teeth—sharp, Pel noticed—his quickening breaths making his voice come more haltingly, choked. It was the same thing Bruant always did when anxious.

It wouldn't do for Kip to panic again, to start crying too hard to speak, not when Pel needed to hear what he had to say. Not when Bruant was in trouble, and they were rapidly running out of time.

Treat him like he's human.

The thought was anathema, but it crossed Pel's mind regardless. Kip looked—mostly—like a scared human youth, barely out of his teenage years. Just like his son. The voice of experience in the back of his mind told him not to buy into appearances, to go upstairs and get his binding amulet, to demand answers. The obvious target for blame was right here. The obvious culprit was right here. A demon was right here.

But he was one damn frightened demon.

Instead of demanding that Kip come closer, Pel went to him, taking a seat on the stool next to the one where Kip's feet rested. Pel sighed, forcing himself to think: *not a demon. Just human. Just a scared kid.*

"Hey," he said softly. "Yeah, I'm mad. But it's because I'm scared for my son. You're scared for him, too, right?"

A shudder passed through Kip's body, and he let out a sound that sounded more like a yowl than a sob, hunching forward with his narrow shoulders tensed almost all the way up to his ears. His hands turned into fists, knotted on his knees.

If he were human, I'd try to comfort him. Pel exhaled slowly, then put a hand on Kip's back. He was hot through his shirt, like he was running a fever. Pel didn't know if that was normal for a demon of his kind, or some kind of reaction to whatever he had with Bruant. If he assumed the latter, maybe he could have more sympathy.

He found that was a little easier than he'd like. "What's your real name, Kip?" he asked gently.

"Please don't call me by my real name," Kip mumbled. "Most demons, I mean, pick a nickname—"

"I know," Pel said. "I'm not going to try to bind you. I promise. But I don't know you. I don't know how Bruant knows you. We need to get along if we're going to be any good to Bruant, right?"

Whatever he did about this demon could happen *after* he got Bruant sorted out. Perhaps Kip would reveal some information Pel could use. Perhaps, instead of Kip damning Bruant further in the Inquisition's eyes, there'd be a way to turn him in that would get Bruant *out*.

Kip trembled under his touch. "Keperat," he said, almost a whisper. "But I use Kip. Please..."

"Okay, Kip," Pel said. "You called yourself a familiar? Is that what type of demon you are?"

"Familiars aren't..." Kip trailed off. "There are a few types that can become familiars. I'm an imp."

Pel rubbed that warm back. The muscles under it felt slightly off, not quite right, but were clearly tense regardless. They relaxed very slightly under his touch. "What do imps do? I don't understand what drew you to Bruant," he added, after the muscles of Kip's shoulders jerked in response, "and without knowing that, I don't know if there's anything that can help us."

"We eat emotions," Kip said. He looked up at Pel with a sudden visible spike of anxiety. "Not all emotions! We all... specialize. I eat anger at oneself."

"That's... very specific," Pel said, knowing he had to respond somehow but drawing a blank.

Kip tensed again, then drew a series of invisible concentric circles with his fingertip on the bar top. "It's... groups," he mumbled, voice a tremulous whine. "We get the most if we feed from our specific area." He retraced the smallest circle. "Anger at oneself." Redrew the next. "Anger." Redrew the last. "Related feelings. Self-hate or guilt. Then we turn it into energy we can give back to the people we share ourselves with."

"Magicians," Pel said, confirming without having to ask. Kip nodded, and Pel sighed, continuing. "In other words, you've been teaching Bruant magic because he's angry enough to feed you."

"That's a little... it's not quite... I guess you can think of it that way..." Kip voice rose in pitch with each word. "He *is* really angry. That's how I noticed him.

And he has the ability—to do magic, I mean—so I... thought he should know. That he could learn if he wanted."

In other words, whether it was true or not, the demon believed, or at least would claim, that it had been Bruant's choice. "What if he stopped being angry ever again? If you ate too much of it."

"It doesn't work like that," Kip said, frowning uncertainly at Pel. "You know that, right? Even if your anger goes away or you run out of energy for it or you resolve it, you can always get angry again later. I think there are some imps who drain people into numbness, but even so, they'll recover eventually. I wasn't hurting him."

"I believe you," Pel said, though he wasn't sure he did. "You haven't drained my anger right now, though."

Kip shook his head, eyes wide. "No," he said, a breathless squeak, shoulders rising slightly as if he were trying to make himself look bigger. "You're scary when you're angry."

Some demon, Pel thought, the thought more wry than bitter. He shook his head, trying to relax, make his posture even less threatening. "So you're saying that no matter what, you could get anger out of him."

"Well... not when he's not angry at the time? But even if he couldn't support me, I could get it from anyone around me who *was* angry," Kip said. "I'd eat some of their energy and convert the rest for my partner. Once a familiar is bonded to their magician, they're bonded until that magician breaks the bond or dies, so it wouldn't matter whether I got it from him or someone else."

Pel felt hope rise up, finally. "So you have a bond

with Bruant! Can you use that to help him—?"

Kip's lower lip trembled. He only restrained it for a couple of seconds before his face crumpled and he began to weep again, although he was clearly fighting it. "He broke it," he choked out, around the tightness of tears. "When they caught me. He broke our bond and told me to run. I don't know what to do! This is the second time. Maybe it's me? Am I just a bad familiar?"

The news settled like a weight into Pel's stomach. He swallowed. "The second time...?" he prompted.

Kip hunched over completely, folding around his knees. "A lady called Vautour called me into the city," he whispered softly. "I was a pretty new demon. I'd never bonded to a person before. I was wandering around the wilderness, crazy hungry, and she called for a familiar, so I climbed the wall as a cat. I don't know how nobody spotted me. But she was taken away by the Inquisition, and she died. She died."

"Kip—"

"I felt it," he said, his whine getting lower, throatier. "*She* didn't dissolve our bond. I felt her die. I've been scared to leave the city again in case they catch me trying to leave. I wandered around as a cat and then I met Bru and I thought, this time I could do it right. This time I could love someone and they'd be okay! But I was *wrong* and he's going to die because of me." He looked up again, eyes brimming with tears and pupils narrowed into slits. "He's going to die because of me, Pel!"

Anger rose in Pel, sharp, as much toward himself as it was toward Kip. He hadn't seen the warning signs. He should have noticed, he should have—but, no, the demon was right.

It *was* because of him. Pel's fists clenched at his

sides with the force of trying to hold his reaction in.

Kip let out another sob, more animal than human, face crumpling again as he bowed his head, shoulders shaking. It looked like he was ready to accept whatever punishment Pel wanted to give him.

And like that, Pel's anger was gone, leaving behind nothing but the exhaustion—just a quiet, sad thing. He didn't know if Kip had gulped his rage down, desperate even in his fear, or if it was just his own empathy for something in pain right in front of him. He wasn't sure it mattered.

"Come on," Pel said softly. He got up, clasping one of Kip's hands and tugging him upright.

"What...?" Kip raised his head again. His face was wet and snot dripped down to his upper lip.

Pel let out a *tsk* and wiped Kip's nose on his sleeve before he let himself think about it. "We need to go see Tari."

"Tari..." Kip nodded suddenly, perking up visibly. "Yeah! Yes, they'll know what to do."

"It might be their fault," Pel warned. "They threatened to tell the Inquisition that Bru had been consorting with demons. I thought they were bluffing, but they might have been serious. And the demon they meant might not have been themself—it might have been you."

"Tari wouldn't," Kip protested, holding Pel's gaze, his own expression earnest. "I really don't think so."

"I hope you're right," Pel said, tired, "because I don't know anyone else in this entire damned city who might help us."

Chapter Seven

Pel dug up the sign he'd made when Bruant had been badly sick a few years earlier, a hastily-scribbled *'Closed until further notice for family reasons'*, and hung it on the door. He looked at it, wondering what people would think when they saw it, then decided that he had far more pressing things on his mind. News would get around—it always did.

He knew better than anybody that nothing in Dolana stayed secret for very long.

He pulled on a heavy cloak. Kip, a cat once more, jumped onto his shoulders, and Pel draped the hood around him so he was hidden from sight.

Still, Pel could feel the weight of him, a heavy press against his neck. *I'm carrying the demon who corrupted my son.* And then, *the demon who cried over him. Shit.* He tried not to think too much about how those two facts pulled him in different directions at once, the anger and grief and sympathy overwhelming and contradictory. He didn't have the time to sort himself out—didn't know if there could *ever* be enough time.

He headed out into the dim evening.

Orphie was none too happy to see him on her doorstep. "I don't want any trouble," she warned, in place of a greeting.

"I don't want any either," he responded, hearing his voice come out rough. "I need to talk to Toutarelle

Walker."

"What do you want her for?" Orphie asked sharply. "I heard you kicked her out. What, does she owe you money? You can damn well come back during the day then."

"Is she in?"

"Get on with you!"

He sighed. "No," he lied. "Actually, I owe *her* money. After our disagreement, she left in such a hurry that I never gave her back her deposit. I just saw it and—and I don't feel right holding onto money that's rightfully hers. I'd like to give it to her, and hopefully an apology with it."

Orphie squinted at him dubiously—or at least, she'd always had a squint, but it was clear she was now making an effort at it. "And that's it? And you aren't thinking of poaching her back for your rooms if you make nice with her again?"

"She's all yours," he said dryly. "Even if we make amends, I doubt either of us want a professional relationship that can be disrupted this easily by an argument."

"Hmm," Orphie said. For a long moment she just glared at him but finally stepped back, holding the door open. "201. If I hear any yelling I'm coming up there with a kitchen knife, mind."

"I'll mind," Pel agreed. He nodded politely as he entered, then headed for the stairs.

Orphie's place was in fine condition, decorated with incongruous paintings of chickens and stitched wall art, more suitable to the old style of a country house than to a city tenement. It was not, Pel thought as he went upstairs, the sort of image that suited Tari at all. But that was probably part of why they had come to Pel's inn first.

He found 201 and knocked. "Tari. I need to speak with you."

Silence.

He knocked again. "Kip's here, too," he added, tired.

After another brief pause, the door opened inward. Tari smiled out at him, seeming completely unoffended at the sight of him. "Well," they said. "Come on in, then."

There was something that looked more delicate and feminine about them today, the softness of their face or the fall of their hair or the set of their shoulders. It was hard for him to put his finger on it exactly, but he doubted it was actually any kind of vulnerability in response to his having hurt their feelings. More likely, they were just trying to keep Orphie's sympathies with them to cover up anything she might find suspicious.

He unfastened his cloak and let Kip hop down. Kip transformed in midair, black shape twisting in a way that almost hurt to look at, before he landed in a crouched human form in front of them both. After a moment, Pel realized with some surprise that Kip had positioned himself directly between Tari and Pel, deliberately—this small, timorous thing was trying to protect one of them from the other.

Uncomfortably, he had a good idea which one of them Kip found more threatening.

Pel gathered up his cloak into a bundled roll, stalling briefly, not quite able to meet Tari's gaze. They waited for him, eyebrows raised, arms crossed.

Slowly, agonizingly, he went down on one knee, then the other, lowering his head, deferential in spite of the chills it gave him to do so. "I'm sorry," he said, voice low, rough. "For what I said before."

Although he couldn't see Tari's expression, his head still bowed, their voice was quite a bit more surprised than he'd expected. "Is that so?" Tari said. Then, with a great deal more sympathy than Pel thought he deserved: "Good gods, man. What's *happened*?"

He swallowed. "Tari, I need you to answer something for me. I want to believe in you. I know you have no reason to think I do, but it's true. I need to know: did you tell the Inquisition anything?"

"What? No." This time the surprise turned into alarm, then a bitterly amused resignation. "What *happened*, Pel? And if Kip's here looking like this, where's Bru?"

He swallowed. Tears rose up, prickling his eyelids. *Shit.* The last thing he wanted to do was cry in front of Tari, but he didn't know if he could hold it back. He supposed it was only fair. If Tari hadn't sold Bruant out, if they *really* hadn't been involved in this, then Pel had nothing to do but beg for their forgiveness and help.

"The Inquisition took him," he managed to say around the lump in his throat, hearing his voice come out muffled and choked. "They caught him practicing magic. Kip took off so they wouldn't have any proof, and came to me even though—I mean, he knows how I feel about demons. But what choice do either of us have right now?"

"Not very much," Tari said, after a brief pause. They came closer, maneuvering around Kip, who swiveled to watch them both. Brown-trousered legs stopped in front of Pel, bare feet below, and Tari slowly came into view as they crouched, gazing at Pel with those blue eyes still terribly bright, expression intrigued. "So now you've come running to me."

There was no vindictiveness in their tone, just a strange sort of curiosity.

"I don't know what to do, Tari!" Kip interrupted. "Bru's gone, he cut me off, they'll be hurting him, they might kill him, he might already be dead and I wouldn't even know, I'm so scared! I'm scared, Tari..." He crawled forward, grabbed their shoulder, and rocked Tari back and forth to get attention.

Tari didn't look at him, gaze focused on Pel. Kip sagged, staring at them with eyes that seemed impossibly large as tears welled up again.

Pel said, in a whisper, "I'm sorry. I said terrible things to you. I was afraid of what you might do. But the worst happened without you having to do a thing. You were innocent—of the things I claimed." He couldn't say they were fully innocent and mean it. *But I don't think Tari'd believe it if I did.* "I don't have anywhere else to turn. Nobody in this city will take on the Inquisition."

"And you think I will?" Tari asked mildly. "In my position?"

"I don't know." Of course not. What demon would put themselves directly in the path of the Inquisition? "But I'm sorry. If you can help me, please. I'll do anything." An idea welled in him, horrific and depressing, repulsive, appalling.

This is for Bruant.

He choked out, "I'll give you my soul, if that's what you want. If that's enough to make it worthwhile for you. Just—*please*."

For a moment, Tari didn't react at all, didn't change in any way; they ignored Pel before them on his knees, his shoulders shaking. Ignored Kip beside them, crouched and crying.

And then they let out an exaggerated sigh, sinking back further until they were seated cross-legged between Pel and Kip.

"Twenty-year-olds are the *worst*," Tari groaned. "I mean, they're great, love them, but they all think they're immortal. I was dating someone around that age back in Potfeld not too long ago, and ended up breaking up with him out of the goodness of my heart. Taking life-threatening risks practically seemed to have become his fetish." They laughed briefly, warm and fond in their reminiscing. "I thought maybe my personality was rubbing off on him."

Frankly, Pel couldn't imagine Tari *dating* anyone, and more importantly, had no idea how this was relevant—until after a moment, realization dawned. "Are you," he said carefully, "considering some kind of life-threatening risk?"

"Not for *your* sake," Tari said dismissively, giving him a once-over with a cool look. "Bruant and Kip, though... I'd like to see them do well for themselves. And besides, rescuing a newly-awakened magician from the Inquisition in a demon-hating city? Sounds terrifying and entertaining. I'm into that."

Pel swallowed the lump in his throat, the aching regret in his chest. He deserved to be dismissed out of hand, he knew that. Tari would think so, at least. He'd doubted them. He'd disrupted their plans.

"Thank you," he said, quiet and overwhelmed, even as fear chilled the blood in his veins, leaving him sweaty and cold at the same time, his palms itching in his anxiety. "Then—how do you... collect?"

Tari stared at him blankly for a moment before

realizing what he meant. "*Oh*, your soul?" They bit their lower lip, an expression halfway between a frown and something strangely coy. "No... I don't think I'll be taking that, not right now. Though I hope you don't think I'm going to forget that you promised it to me. But you need to be alive if you want to rescue your son, don't you?"

Relief flooded him, its waves lapping at the fear he hadn't lost. He just had to focus on Bruant, he tried to tell himself. *I've made this choice. It's done now.* "Then—"

"But..." Tari interrupted, raising one finger, and some practiced confidence, some deliberate construction, vanished. That vulnerable, softer look seemed to come about them again as they exhaled, head falling forward a bit, gaze dropping. The expression was simultaneously diffident and enticing. "I'm starving."

"What?" Pel asked, startled.

"I haven't fed in days," Tari said. "I'm not *dying*— I'm not that badly off—but I've gone into, hmm. It's a state where I conserve energy. I can go a long time on this if I'm just watching out for myself. But I'm not going to be able to do too much for others on short notice." They looked up again, eyes meeting Pel's, the expression in them starting to warm up again. It was, weirdly, a relief to see. "In a city like this, it takes at least some care to seduce people. I can't just walk up to a stranger and say, 'I'm a cubant, want to play'. But I assume you want to act as soon as possible."

Heart sinking, disgust rising in him—at himself, not Tari, for what he'd done, what he was thinking of doing—he said, "Yes. The longer we take, the worse off Bruant will be."

"Then I need a human volunteer to give me at least a little," Tari said, and spread their hands. "Where do you suggest I get something like that?"

Pel swallowed. Arousal was already racing through him at the thought, and horror along with it. He wanted Tari—hadn't stopped wanting Tari—but knew, now, what Tari was. He tried to imagine giving up parts of himself so some demon could eat him piecemeal, tried to imagine himself *enjoying* it.

No. No way. I can't. I won't. I—

"Kip," he said, much more calmly than he felt. "Go outside."

Kip opened his mouth to protest, then shut it with an audible snap, eyes widening more. He gave them both a long, distressed look, then turned, stalking to the window and transforming as he leapt out. He landed on the ledge outside with a soft thump, ears flattened against his head.

Pel shut the window behind him, drawing the blinds and ignoring Kip's baleful look at him before they closed. "We'll have to keep it quick," he said stiffly, turning back. "Bruant's in danger—"

And then his words cut off because the Tari he was looking at now was different than the Tari he'd been speaking to just moments earlier.

A spade-tipped tail wound around behind them, resting on the floor where they were still sitting, hands splayed in their lap. Their horns went up in a *V*, twisting midway, holding their long dark curls back from their face. Their limbs had lengthened in some hard-to-define way, made more noticeable by how their legs were angled backward with high, deer-like angles leading down to cloven hooves. And those blue eyes had horizontally slit pupils, goatlike.

This was a demon. A cubant.

They grinned, showing too many teeth, and rose from the floor in one fluid, unnervingly graceful motion. Approaching the bed, they held a hand out to Pel, beckoning.

"Come here, Pel," Tari said. It was still their normal voice with no change, startling in its familiarity.

Fear almost overwhelmed Pel's inadvertent arousal—fear, and a gut-deep sense of rejection. Doing this ran counter to everything he believed in, everything he thought was right, everything he'd done in the name of that goal.

It was just Tari, he reminded himself. And then: *But this* is Tari.

Abruptly, Tari laughed, rueful, and rubbed their face with their hands. "I'm scaring you," they said. "Seriously. Oh, Pel. Am I the first demon you've really seen since that aluga?"

His heart gave an unpleasant flop. "There was Kip," he said, tightening his jaw in an attempt to seem dismissive.

"Kip's just an imp," Tari said gently. "Just a little impulse. Hardly the archetypal demon, hm?"

"And cubants are the... archetype?"

"Cubants are," Tari agreed immediately. "Absolutely. We interact with humans more than any other kind, because we prefer you alive and well."

Alive and well was one way to put how he was feeling. He wanted them, both physically and just... who they were. It didn't matter to his body that they were a demon, and it bothered the rest of him less than he wished it did, but it *should*. He knew that. It should bother him more than anything else in the world.

"I feel like I'm betraying Phalene," he blurted out.

Tari's eyes widened. He realized with a shock that they hadn't realized what they were asking of him, how much the past still stuck with him. And why should they? He hadn't said much about it at all. "Oh, Pel," Tari said again, soft.

He tried to explain, to find words. "And—and Bruant. He's hurting right now, he's—"

To his surprise, Tari moved back a little, giving him space. "Pel..." They paused, as if searching for words, a faint line appearing between their creased brows. "You're scared and hurting, so let me—just let me talk for a moment, we don't need to jump into anything here. Look, I don't want your soul. I certainly wasn't expecting you to offer it, so I might as well rescind your offer for you."

He blinked, eyes widening. "What—?"

Tari shrugged. "Honestly, the human soul is a powerful thing, but I'd rather see what a person does with theirs intact. So there's that. And about sex—"

Pel had started to relax. He stiffened again, looking them over: a demon he should reject, but everything he wanted right now. "Yes?"

"If it's a betrayal to sleep with me, then we can do less than that," Tari said simply. They held out a hand again, coaxing him closer. "I am what I am, and I'm not going to apologize for it. Everything needs to eat. But I can see this is important to you, and I don't want to force you to do anything you don't want. Kissing alone won't do as much good for me, but it's better than nothing. I don't need much sexual energy to have some to spare on other things."

They're being too nice. The mix of emotions almost overwhelmed him. Fear and panic, still there.

Revulsion, relief, guilt, longing, grief. He blinked rapidly, trying to blink the tears away before they formed. "If we start I don't know if I can stop," he said. "Even if I want to. I haven't... for a long time and you're very—"

"I'm very much a cubant," Tari agreed wryly. "I know the effect I have."

Pel said, choked, "I don't see any other options."

"I know." They stayed where they were, reaching out to him, not otherwise moving. "I don't like it to be that way. If you can't do this, I can try to hunt and hope that works. I can't get my energy from Kip or I would, Pel."

His lips twisted. "That's... unreliable."

"It is," Tari agreed. "If you're willing to work with me, I'll stop it if we go too fast. Trust me a little?"

"I can't—"

"Can you try?" Tari asked.

Fuck. Pel let out a shudder. "I can try," he said, and finally took those last few steps closer, taking their hand, letting them pull him down onto the bed.

Tari relaxed back easily. Pel didn't know how they could—*won't their tail make lying down uncomfortable?* he thought inanely—but perhaps he was just reading his own discomfort into Tari. He hesitated over them, one arm braced next to their body, stiff, all muscles tight as he held himself up.

Slowly, Tari raised their arms, sliding hands up Pel's sides until they reached his ribs, then moving up from there, slow and firm, to touch his back instead. Something about the gesture, gentle and almost cautious, sent a shudder through Pel.

He hadn't ever considered bedding a demon in much detail, but even so, he had never thought it could be quite so—nice. Exhaling sharply, he folded down against Tari, bracketed by their arms, their long legs, bent at the knee.

Tari let out an approving murmur in response, smiling at him, hands sliding to cup the back of Pel's neck. "You feel nice," they said, a dreamy murmur. Their eyes were half-closed and their pupils had expanded enough to make them almost seem black. "Kiss me?"

The simple request—the fact that it *was* a request—sent a helpless rush of arousal through Pel. He swallowed abruptly, convulsive, around a throat that no longer wanted to work the way it should. "Tari—"

Tari's fingers rubbed against the short, spiky hairs against at the base of Pel's skull. The pointed tip of their tongue touched their lower lip, and the sight of it, wet and pink and not at all the right shape, sent another shock through him.

I want to taste that. I want to feel it. He let himself think that, exploring the thought for a few dizzying, uncomfortable moments as he stared at Tari's tongue, their lips—and then lowered his head, urgently pressing his mouth to theirs.

Under him, Tari groaned softly, lips moving against his, mouth opening, and then they were kissing. Pel let himself feel it, feel a hot body against his, *Tari's* body against his, shifting and wanting. He let himself want this, want to feel, touch, have, and, with a shudder, he let himself move in return, rolling against them.

It was impossible to keep track of the time passing even with his helpless awareness of how little time the two of them had. The careful, exploratory passes of their lips turned quickly into something more biting, desperate. He ate at Tari's mouth like he was the one planning to devour them instead of the other way around, nipped at their lower lip and dragged his teeth before crushing their mouths together with renewed passion.

Tari was sucking breaths in every time their kiss broke even briefly. He could feel the hard pressure of Tari's arousal against his hip, a strangely nostalgic sensation. It wouldn't be the first time; he'd slept with a few men when he was younger, and had dated a woman in the guard who was taking medicine to better match her looks to her heart back when they'd been in training together. The sensation was strange only from how long it had been since he'd felt anything of another person's pleasure, let alone a particular one he'd put behind him when he had fallen for Phalene.

Not to mention that it was with a demon. Knowing he was deliberately bringing pleasure to someone who fed from it was heady and terrifying.

He shifted slightly to make it easier for Tari to grind, shuddering as he pressed a thigh against their legs. Clearly pleased by his reaction, Tari squirmed under him as they shifted to touch more, hands hungry and roaming, hips rocking for more pressure, more friction, *more—*

I want to feel good, Pel thought dazedly. *I want to feel—*

He broke the kiss to start mouthing down Tari's throat, mapping out the long, elegant curve with lips and teeth. Even though there was no reason for it beyond some mimicry of human desire, he could feel a flutter of pulse against his lips.

"Hey—" Tari said, a soft moan as they tilted their head back.

They didn't sound like they wanted Pel to stop, so he didn't, straddling one of Tari's thighs so he could free up a hand and run it over one of Tari's small pointed breasts, down to a hip, back up again. He sucked and bit at Tari's throat again, earning a gasp as Tari arched, tugging at his hair.

"Hey," they said again, more pointedly. "Nnh, Pel..."

Pel didn't listen. Didn't want to listen, didn't want to let what he was doing catch up with him. Didn't want to have to start thinking about it again. He found the hem of Tari's shirt, slid his fingers up underneath. He couldn't get farther than the bottom of Tari's rib cage with their vest still buttoned, but regardless, he was touching skin: soft, warm skin, smooth and inviting—

Tari pulled at Pel's hair roughly enough to yank his head back. "*Hey.*"

Pel sucked air, flushed and anxious with desire and wondering why, when Tari was so clearly enjoying this, he'd been stopped. "What?"

"You didn't want to go too far," Tari reminded him, breathless and a little pouty. "You said this'd be a betrayal."

Shit. "I don't want to stop *now*," he muttered, looking somewhere around their throat instead of at their face.

Tari groaned, the sound both disappointed and erotic as they dropped their head back to the pillow. "Will you have wished you stopped," they said, strained, "later? I told you to trust me."

That made Pel pause, the question helping him clear his head a little. *Fuck. Later. Fuck.* He swallowed with his throat gone dry, and slowly sat back, almost peeling himself away from the heat of Tari's body. Their lips were swollen and reddened, cheeks flushed, eyes hazy, and they looked annoyed—at themself, he thought, not at him.

"Why would you stop me when you want me to give it to you?" he asked, dazed.

"Because I'm a fucking good person," Tari snapped, and unwound their arms from Pel, blowing hair out of their face with an annoyed huff. "And I respect your feelings for your dead wife."

Pel stared at them.

"I," he began, and then the guilt hit.

His dead wife. His dead, demon-slain wife. He'd lived this long, lived fourteen years with that anger, that hatred. No demon was an exception, because it could have been any of them to do it. How could it not be, if the first one that she met ended up murdering her?

But the guilt wasn't just toward that. It was in the realization of the lie. He would have willingly sacrificed himself on the altar of his own lust, lacking the ability to stop for his own sake once he got started.

And Tari—Tari hadn't let him.

Then there was Kip: open and honest and an emotional wreck and he'd been that way as a cat, too, clingy and sad and needy. He'd needed Bruant, and Bruant had needed *him*. So much of Bruant's life had started to revolve around that cat, that companion, giving him something to turn to when he could no longer face Pel. Kip was a support for him. But still, a predator. Both of those at the same time.

Demons were *all* predators—that was still true. That was undeniably true. They wouldn't have even found themselves in this situation, this weird dance of consent and guilt and necessity, if Tari didn't need to feed off humans. Kip did, too. And they were just coincidentally both demons who fed on human emotions, which could seem harmless enough, but there were others who fed on flesh, minds—

I just don't know anymore. Maybe some of those were careful too. Maybe *predator* meant nothing more than *dangerous*.

And humans could be dangerous, too—to demons and each other. *He'd* been preying on the people in this city, encouraging them to trust him while watching for openings to turn them in. He hadn't wanted to hurt anybody—had wanted to *protect* people—but Bruant had been right. It was hypocritical to behave like a protector while ensuring people would get hurt.

Bruant had hated that, both on its own merits and because he hadn't wanted Pel to hurt anyone for his sake. Bruant wouldn't want him to continue now, either, not past what he wanted to do, even if it would make it easier to rescue him. Bruant would never put himself before others.

He'd been using Bruant as an excuse, using *Phalene* as an excuse, when really the only person responsible was himself.

"Pel—?"

He'd gotten up without realizing it, stumbling away from the bed and scrubbing his hands roughly over his face. The guilt felt like a palatable cloud around him, like he could taste and smell and feel it. His wife's ghost hanging around him, Bruant's condemnation hanging around him, his own stubborn refusal to *see* hanging around him, a cloud of confusion mixing in a stomach-churning stench.

"Fuck." The arousal still rushing through him with every breath made it even worse. He had to do something. He couldn't stay here, but he couldn't think— "Where's the toilet?"

"Next door," Tari said. Then, with a strained, sympathetic smile and a tone like they were trying to lighten the mood, "Mind if I lean on the other side of the wall while I wait for you?"

It didn't work. *They know what I'm going to do. Shit. Really?* He was aroused to the point of pain, nauseated with it. Of course a cubant would know.

"Do what you want," he said, more implicit permission than he wanted to let himself think about, and fled.

~~*

He returned sooner than he'd like, red-faced and unnaturally tired, with water dripping from his hair after he'd splashed his face from the tap. Tari had opened the window sometime recently and Kip was back inside, looking about as embarrassed and anxious as Pel felt.

"Uh," Pel said, then decided that he didn't want to explain himself or, in fact, anything at all, and just sat on the bed with Tari like nothing had happened. He tried to find whatever *lack* was in himself after feeding them, and found nothing but the vague sluggishness that he'd normally write off as exhaustion from a day like today. He cleared his throat. "So. Did that help?"

"It *definitely* helped," Tari said, smiling at him with a small shrug. Their hair slid aside and he saw that the mark he'd tried to leave on their throat was already gone.

He wasn't sure how he felt about that.

They clearly misunderstood the look on his face. "Don't worry too much," Tari added. "It's only enough that I feel like it wouldn't be blatantly suicidal to take on an entire anti-demon brigade, anyway. Just *mostly* suicidal."

Pel let out a breath. They weren't odds he liked, but they were the odds that they had. "We need to get him out of the city," he said, low-voiced. "There's nowhere safe to hide him once we get him out of the Inquisition building. I don't have any friends who'd be willing to stick their necks out if the Inquisition came knocking, and the bar will be the first place they'd look. Even assuming we were able to get him out of his cell in the first place."

"Sneaking him out the city gates is too much of a long shot," Tari said. "Having come in through one, I'd assume the others are pretty much the same?"

"Pretty much," Pel said. "I was thinking we'd have to go over the wall. I know the patrols well enough to know their timing gaps—that'd be the safest bet." He dropped his gaze, unable to keep eye contact with them. "But I don't know that it'll work. After we break him out, the patrols won't stick to their normal rhythm. They'll start combing the area for likely escape routes. And they'd alert volunteers, too. The city would be up our asses in under a quarter hour, even this late at night."

"We can move fast," Kip said, determinedly. "As long as we get to the other side of the wall, it's fine, right? We won't be their problem anymore and anyway. They don't go out there."

"We're not all as fast as cats," Pel said, a little cranky. "And us humans need actual food to eat.

There's a lot of wilderness between here and the next city. We'd need to bring supplies with us, so it's not as simple as just getting out with nothing but the clothes on our backs."

Tari held up a hand. "I've got an idea forming. Give me a minute to think it through."

Pel stared at Tari as they closed their eyes, frowning, a line between their brows, and took the moment to study them, feeling a strange rush of gratitude. There was no sign of hesitation in Tari's pose, no resentment or regret for being dragged into this.

Tari opened their eyes again, the horizontal pupils narrowed to a line. "Okay," they said, tone firm. "Let's try this."

And then they were changing—hair swirling around them as it pulled itself up to become short, shoulders broadening, even their stance shifting to something more solid. Pel gaped as he abruptly found himself facing a perfect copy of himself, down to the scars on his cheek.

The other Pel winked at him, smirking.

Pel's mouth worked a few times as he stared at them. Tari had mimicked his appearance with an uncanny accuracy, from height and weight to smaller details. The fine worry lines on his forehead were there, as was the slight bend of his nose from where it had been broken years earlier, and the small mole at the corner of his left eye. They had matched the light brown of his skin perfectly, and copied his hair not only in style or length but, he thought, perhaps even perfectly representing the smattering of gray throughout his hair. In appearance alone, it was like staring into a mirror.

But they had shifted to lean on one hip again, hand planted there, grinning slyly. In Pel's voice, they asked, "Not bad, hm, sweetheart?"

"I don't talk like that," he managed, through his shock, and heard it come out awkward, like his tongue was too thick. "I don't *stand* like that."

"You don't, do you?" Tari mused. "Then let's try this again." They straightened, shoulders back, and crossed their arms across their chest instead. "Listen up, soldiers," they barked.

Kip giggled.

"I don't talk like *that* either," Pel protested, flustered, and Tari flashed him an unnervingly charming smile. *Shit. My dimples really are devastating*, he found himself thinking, and almost got dizzy with confusion.

"All right," Tari said, and this time, the tone of their voice was unnervingly accurate. They relaxed a little, a perfect mimicry of Pel's usual stance. "Enough joking around. Here's what I'm thinking..."

Chapter Eight

Somehow the plan ended up with Pel alone, filling two packs as heavily as he thought they could carry on a journey by foot, and wondering how it had come to the point where he had to leave rescuing his own son to a pair of demons while he dithered over what parts of his life to bring along in a bag.

But Tari's idea was the best that any of them had managed, especially on short notice.

Tari would transform into a copy of Pel, mimicking his mannerisms and speech patterns as they had previously demonstrated. Kip, under "Pel's" cloak, would go with them up to the door. Tari would use their aura of attraction to become more persuasive while begging to talk to Bruant, while Kip drained the guards' anger at "Pel's" intrusion to make them even more susceptible.

Then, while "Pel" talked to Bruant, Kip would reestablish a bond, letting him pour energy into and through Bruant. He could use this to briefly obscure the scene while Tari embraced Bruant and transformed into Bruant instead, transferring the cloak and Kip to allow them to essentially switch places.

"The obscuring won't do much," Kip had warned. "Because he won't know the spell. I can force it through him but it'll just cause a little misdirection. Make it easier for them to see what they're looking for instead of what's actually happening."

"That's fine," Tari had said in Pel's deep voice, eyes glittering in a way that Pel was fairly certain his own eyes did not. "A real spell has a higher risk of setting off their wards, anyway. A bit of energy just focused on causing confusion is more likely to fly under the radar."

After that, Tari, now "Bruant", would refuse to help, and the real Bruant, being fed energy by Kip to keep him going no matter how badly off he was, and still obscured so people would be more likely to confuse him for Pel, would storm out. The two of them would then go to meet up with Pel and escape over the wall to safety.

And in the meantime, Tari would sit in the cell, pretending to be Bruant and buying time for them to be well away from the city. It wouldn't take long, because they wouldn't need to go far—as Kip had noted, the guards were reluctant to leave the city, and would hardly walk several hours out in a random direction to catch people they'd want gone anyway, especially if they wouldn't even be sure at first that they'd left the city. So after a few hours, Tari would transform into a shape that could get out of the cell and slip away.

It was a plan, but not exactly the most foolproof, which meant Pel's mind was helpfully outlining all the ways it could go wrong.

From the start, Tari and Kip could get turned away. Or they could get in, and the wards could reveal them for what they really were before they even got to Bruant. The inquisitors might demand he take the cloak off. The obscuring could fail or Bruant could be too badly off to pretend to be Pel without warning.

The warding could prevent Tari from transforming into Bruant. They might be detained on the way out. Tari might not be able to slip out later.

Even for his own part, if the guards had changed their routine at all, or if Kip and Bruant were held up, or if he somehow missed their approach, he might get caught loitering and not be able to clear an escape for all of them.

He'd expressed this to Tari, of course.

"Well," Tari had said, giving Pel an expression so doubting that he thought at once he might come to hate his own face, "I could just murder everyone in the building instead and break him out that way?"

"What? No!" Pel had stared at them. "I've known these people my entire life, Tari!"

"Then the riskier option it is," Tari had said, and grinned. "I'll save the other one for a backup plan."

So as Pel lurked behind a tree, sweating half his body weight out and straining to make out any unexpected movement on the pathway leading past this section of old wall, he wished he was, perhaps, a little less moral and a little less attached. *There's no way this haphazard plan could ever work.*

There was nobody more surprised than him that it did.

Exactly around the time they'd hoped, even though they'd had only a vague guess of how long things would take, a pair of people approached. They were moving through the shadows, the smaller one supporting the other beneath a too-large cloak.

They've done it. Pel had to use all his will in order not to break from his own hidden position and run over, fearing that would be too obvious, but his throat swelled tight and his eyes stung. Finally, when they were close enough that it would no longer risk undoing everything they'd worked for, he reached out to touch Bruant's shoulder.

Bruant startled violently, his cloak falling back from his hair, and Pel stared at him in silence for a moment. There was a massive bruise at the corner of Bruant's mouth, but it already looked old. Kip, too, had kept his part of the deal, and was forcing Bruant to heal faster than his body would normally manage. Bruant stared back at Pel, silent and unsure. His eyes were completely wild, white showing all the way around the irises.

It wasn't that he didn't recognize his father. He did—but in doing so, feared he'd escaped the Inquisition only to fall into the hands of one more judge.

Worse than that, though, worse than seeing Bruant afraid of *him*, was something else in that expression. Something was wrong there that Pel couldn't place, unhinged and hurt, like a wounded animal on the brink of fight or flight.

Still, given what he'd just been through, it was no surprise.

"I'm so glad you're alive," Pel whispered, and carefully pulled Bruant into an embrace.

Bruant winced at the first touch, half in physical pain and half in some kind of terrified anticipation—then let out a sob, beginning to tremble violently. Pel started to pull back, not wanting to trap him, but then Bruant's arms came around him in return, unsteady but firm.

They held each other tightly for a few precious seconds, both shaking, and then, reluctantly, Pel drew back. "We don't have long." The guards would be by again soon; they needed to get to the wall and over it. "Did Kip explain?"

Bruant nodded, eyes too-wide and tears clumping his lashes together. "Dad, I—"

"Not now. When we're away."

Kip put his arms around both of them. He was incredibly warm, as though all the energy he'd been pouring into Bruant in the course of this plan had overheated him, like a lamp left burning too long. "We have to hurry," he agreed. "I'm going first."

Pel studied Bruant again, anxious and mindful of his son's well-being, then turned to watch as Kip took a run at the wall and then *up* it, hands and feet not even seeming to need the footholds that Pel had confirmed were there. He reached the top in seconds, then turned around, pressing his stomach to the edge as he dug his knees into the rough stone of the top and held his hands down.

"Come on," Pel said. He led Bruant over to the wall, with a quick look around to make sure the guards weren't in sight yet, and twined his hands together, making a stirrup for Bruant.

Bruant hesitated, wobbling briefly without support, but then his look of uncertainty firmed up. Pel grinned a little, half-rueful, half-proud.

Yeah. There's no option here. You've just got to be able to do it.

Leaning on the wall, Bruant hopped and got one foot into the cup of Pel's hands. He reached up as far as he could, grabbing a double handful of the rough-hewn rock.

"One—two—" Pel began. On "*Three!*" he shoved up as hard as he could, at the same time Bruant hauled himself up. For a moment he was unbalanced, almost airborne, hands off the wall and reaching up toward Kip.

Kip grabbed on, hands locking around Bruant's wrists, letting out a whine of effort as he hauled Bruant up. Bruant's feet scrabbled on the wall until they found footholds. He was pulled more than he climbed, but made it to the top, balanced unsteadily next to Kip, clinging to him and breathing hard.

Bruant looked drawn with pain even in this pale light, shuddering with it, and anger rushed through Pel at both the Inquisition and himself for having let it come to this. *I don't have time for regret*, he reminded himself. *I need to stay calm, we're not out of this yet—* but he remembered Kip and let himself feel it.

Someone might as well get something out of this.

As he looked up at Kip, their eyes met and the anger drained away. Even knowing that he'd been offering it up, he couldn't be sure if it really was Kip accepting the reward, or if his impulse to push it down and focus had taken over. But Kip smiled at him and, surprising himself, Pel couldn't help but smile back.

Next were the packs. He tossed them up to Kip one at a time, a quick hand-off before Kip dropped them over the other side. Despite their speed, it still felt like it was all taking far too long. Pel wiped his sweating palms off on the legs of his pants, then grabbed the rock and climbed.

It was just as well he'd given it a test run earlier; it was dark and he was tired and nervous. But he'd made climbs like this dozens of times, and got to the top with only a couple of scares. Once he reached it, he was grabbed by both Kip and Bruant, the latter struggling a little and letting go as soon as Pel was balanced.

Sitting on the top, he could see both the city

stretching away on the left and the wilderness stretching away on the right. It was unnerving, a strange split between the reality of the life he'd lived so far and the reality of the life he was going to live from now on. Time was ticking. If he hesitated any longer, the guards would come into sight. The three of them would be terribly visible up on the wall, backlit by the moon—

"Hey." Kip butted Pel's shoulder with his forehead. "You gotta get down first so I can lower Bru to you."

He went.

Through some miracle, they made it in time. On the other side of the wall, he could hear the guards walking past, talking together, but they hadn't seen or heard anything. There was no sound of disturbance. Tari had, it seemed, pulled off their part well.

And so they were free.

Chapter Nine

At first they walked in silence, finding their way to the nearby river and then following it—or, rather, *Pel* stayed silent. He didn't want to talk, and wasn't sure what he'd say. They were outside—out of the city. The sounds of nature and the scent of fresh air and the weird silence of the forest around the river were unnerving, overwhelming.

But Kip and Bruant were pressed so closely together that they made one shadow, talking in low, hushed murmurs. It reminded Pel of when Kip was a cat, always clinging to Bruant's legs and heels, winding around him as he walked; this just seemed to be the human-shaped equivalent of the same.

From the bits of the conversation that Pel was picking up, Kip was trying to teach Bruant a proper healing spell. Kip's voice was affectionate and a little whiny, despite his teacherly cadence. Bruant, in turn, was finally beginning to relax, like that needy tone was somehow soothing.

Pel, feeling a little like he was witnessing something private—something not *for* him, borderline intimate and borderline anathema—didn't dare interrupt.

Still, eventually, they too lapsed into a companionable silence. Not long after that, Bruant fell back a little to walk alongside Pel, awkward, his shoulders hunched and his gaze downcast.

"Dad?" he said finally, the word blurted too quickly after a long pause. He winced.

"Bru?" Pel asked back, hearing his own voice come out hoarse and exhausted. It had been such a long night already. He pushed past that, reaching out to find Bruant's hand with his own.

Bruant startled, then squeezed it hard, though even that determined grip felt weak. He made a few false starts at talking, more noises than words, then looked down, staring at his feet with eyes that didn't seem to actually be seeing anything. "Are you mad at me?"

"...Mad?" Pel echoed blankly.

Bruant's gaze jerked up at him, stunned by that mild reaction. He gestured in the air with a free hand helplessly, then let it fall. "I really was consorting with demons," he pointed out, unsteady. "I've been learning magic. Everything they accused me of was true. Everything you've hated all this time, everyone you've turned in, I'm one of them. I really am. Kip says I could be a real magician. I have the power. He says I probably got it from my mom, because you don't have any—" He couldn't seem to stop his babbling, free hand grabbing at the air like he could find the words and stuff them back inside himself.

Watching that, Pel's heart ached. "Of course it would be from Phalene," he murmured, sighing. "Listen—"

"And I love Kip, Dad," Bruant added in a rush, saying it more like an apology than anything else. A confession to wrongdoing.

Pel took that in, turned it over, and found himself shrugging it off. If Bruant had to be a magician, then it was just as well that it was Kip who was his partner.

Kip would take care of him. And, thinking back over the events of the night, he thought it might not be so bad to have Kip around, whiny and clingy as he was.

He tried to find a way to articulate all of it, to encompass everything Bruant had said, and just squeezed Bruant's hand again. "Okay," he said. "That's all okay. I love you."

"Okay," Bruant said back, voice high and wobbling. "So you're not mad."

"I'm just glad you're alive," Pel said. It was clear that Bruant needed him to say more, though he didn't know if he had the words, so he drew a breath and struggled forward. "It's not a life I'd have chosen for you, but I didn't have a clear head about that, either. Your mother's death hurt me badly. But that's not your fault. It's not Kip or Tari's faults either. Who knows? Maybe your mother had wanted—had *needed* to be a magician too, and didn't know it. Maybe that's why she always longed for something *more*, something I couldn't give her."

Bruant was staring at him, silent.

Pel swallowed. "It's okay that you've kept secrets. It's not like you could talk to me about these things, not while I've been like this." He hesitated again. "Are *you* mad at me?"

Finally, Bruant made a choked sound. Pel didn't look to see if he were crying again, just held his hand tightly, rubbing the side of it with his thumb. "I'm not mad," Bruant said, voice trembling. "Thanks. Sorry."

"I'd understand if you were," Pel said, and smiled wearily at him. "But I want to do better by you. I don't want you to get hurt ever again, by me or anyone else. Okay?"

Bruant's gaze was almost uncomprehending, but

after a moment, he managed a smile. It was a little weird, and on the verge of collapse, but he seemed to mean it—the expression reached his eyes. "I'd like that, too."

He didn't offer more, and Pel didn't ask for it. He just squeezed Bruant's hand and walked with him until Bruant stepped away first, stumbling at a faster pace to catch up with Kip again.

Pel's hand felt empty, and he went back to checking his pocket watch regularly to distract himself. Soon enough, it told him they'd walked their suggested three hours, so they paused to set up camp.

Bruant nearly collapsed, groaning as he sank down to sit on a log. Kip, still in human form, crawled to and curled up next to him, resting his head in Bruant's lap. Pel found somewhere else to look and give them their privacy as they rested and waited for Tari to catch up.

But Tari didn't.

~~*

"They're too late," Kip said. He'd started pacing the boundaries of their temporary encampment, hair fluffed up with his frustration and worry.

Bruant was huddled in Pel's cloak, looking like he needed about ten more years of sleep than he was likely to get tonight, but also seeming to have himself a lot more together. He said, tentatively, "It hasn't been that long..."

Kip shook his head furiously. If he'd been in his feline form, his tail would be lashing.

"It has," Kip insisted. "Even with how little energy they have right now, Tari can move much, *much* faster than we can. Cubants are *real* shapeshifters. They can turn into anything that any human they've met is attracted to! Even in their imaginations. Lots of people have fantasized all kinds of things. Formless shapes. Things with wings. Things that run fast, too."

They both looked at him dubiously. "I can't say that I've ever fantasized about formless winged things," Pel volunteered.

Even as he said it, he remembered abruptly that he'd spent a few years wishing centaurs existed, combining the best of swift horses and attractive people. He deeply wished that memory had remained buried.

"Um." Kip stopped pacing, turning to face them. "I may be new as demons go, but I'm pretty sure. Not you, but in general. The things people get angry or guilty at themselves over are pretty wild sometimes. You're... you're both doing it right now, actually."

"I am *not*," Pel protested.

Bruant let out a weak laugh and held out an arm. "Come here," he said. "Try to relax."

Pel watched as Kip gazed at Bruant, then sagged in place, as though the tension had just rushed out of him. He padded over to sit next to Bruant, pressing against his side. Bruant turned to brush his lips against Kip's hair and inhaled.

"You two said the rest of the plan went off fine," Pel said. "Kip, *you* were able to get in and out."

"Yeah," Kip said, seemingly unaffected by Bruant huffing him. "The amount of anti-demon wards up were amazing, but they weren't pointed at me or Tari, and the people there opened the doors for us along the way so none of the sealing wards were active. But maybe once those doors were closed, Tari couldn't go out after? Maybe, once they thought Tari was Bruant, the wards were aimed at them. Maybe even just being in that building drained their energy. They didn't have a lot." Kip let out a hiss of breath and dragged his claws along the log they were sitting on. "Maybe, maybe, maybe."

"Tari told me they were strong against that kind of warding," Pel said slowly. "That all cubants were. They got in through the city gates no problem."

"City gates are designed for passage," Bruant said, half-muffled by Kip's hair. "Even if they're made to test for demons along the way, the reason there's a gate so people *can* go in and out. That might be a bit different from magic on a place designed to keep people in and t-torture them."

Kip made a small noise of sympathetic pain, rubbing his cheek against Bruant's. Even so, he kept speaking. "Mm... cubants are different from a lot of demons. They're made to use a connection between bodies. So they're strong against magics that work on the spirit 'cause they're really... fleshy? But even if Tari's strong against it, how strong do you have to be? If one of those problems are true? If all are? Tari fed a lot at the bar 'cause they weren't feeding deep enough for their prey to notice, I bet. And then went without for *days*."

I'd been so proud of that fact, Pel thought, exhausted.

"And I'd think that if the Inquisition ever wanted to hold demons, or even well-trained magicians," Bruant said slowly, tone anxious as he pulled away from Kip a little to face Pel, "they would ward the cells against transformation. They're only effective as "cells" when closed, so they might have been able to transform into me because the doors were still open then. But that means that once I was gone, the Inquisition could do to Tari whatever they did to *me*." His eyes were dark, haunted.

"Only if the door was closed," Pel said firmly, trying to reassure him through confidence alone. He didn't have anything else going for him. "The inquisitors would have to open it to get in to question them."

"But like I'm saying! Tari was already low energy, so they might not be able to do things even then," Kip said. "You two didn't even really sleep together..."

Pel went red. "How do you—"

"You feel guilty about it," Kip said, kind of strained.

Bruant dropped his face into Kip's shoulder. "Can we not?"

"*Anyway*," Pel said forcefully. "How do you even know all this about cubants and so on? I thought you were new. Maybe you're just... misunderstanding?"

Kip shrugged, awkward. "Demons know demon things," he said. "We don't have childhoods or grow up, so we don't learn like humans do. Besides, I ran into plenty of other demons out here before getting called into the city."

Shit. He was out of arguments. Things had gone so well that he'd wanted to hope—but the more they talked, the worse it looked.

He rose and said, "You two, keep walking and following the river. Rest when you have to. There's no need to take it at a fast pace, since they don't even know you're gone. Bru, can you carry my bag while Kip carries the other?"

"Yeah, but—" Bruant looked up at him in wide-eyed alarm. "Dad, you're not going *back*."

"I'll be fine," Pel told Bruant, hoping he wasn't lying. "I've known these people for years."

"But what if—"

"Bru," Pel said. He came over, dropping a hand on Bruant's head. "Tari risked themself for you, because I begged them to. So let me do this for them."

"I can come— "

Pel shook his head. "A second Bruant would give things away for sure. And anyway, they want *you*. Stay out here. Trust your old man."

Bruant stared at him, then lowered his eyes. "We'll keep walking," he said, and took Kip's hand, squeezing it. "But don't you die. I'm not ready to be an orphan. And I'm really not done with you yet."

"I'll do my best," Pel said, the most honest answer he could give.

~~*

It occurred to him, as he made the long walk back, that nobody would actually *know* if he left Tari there. It was a strange, horrible thought that welled up in him, nauseatingly tempting. The plan—*Tari's* plan—had been to put Tari in the cell; it was up to them to escape on their own. If Pel changed his mind on this, all he'd have to do was lie to Bruant and Kip, say that he'd tried but it was too late. It might *actually* be too late if Tari hadn't managed to escape already. He could be walking right back into the maw of danger with the Inquisition alerted, leaving his son fatherless, with only a young demon for company in the wilderness, the two of them with nowhere to go.

Tari would never have asked him to come back for them.

Tari would never have expected him to *want* to.

Pel shook his head, disgusted at himself, as he

stopped at the foot of the wall. He checked his pocket watch, calculating the time until it would absolutely be free from guards again. *Fuck it.* There was nothing in the world he could do to make up for the people he'd betrayed, and he wasn't going to pretend there was, but this was different. He was just *tired* of it. He didn't want to be someone who sold people out anymore, he didn't want to lie to Bruant anymore and, fuck, he just plain wanted Tari back.

It was that simple.

Dawn had already passed before he made it back over the wall. His feet were aching and he needed sleep more than he ever had in his life, but he forced his tired legs to keep going. He strode through the city with an air like he'd gone out for a morning walk to clear his head, and walked right up to the Inquisition building door, as he imagined Tari had done earlier when pretending to be him.

He knocked.

The guard who opened the small windowed slot in the door was a man named Verrat. They recognized each other at once, from all the free drinks Pel had bought him when he'd stopped in on his rounds. The pity on his face was that of a man who knew his acquaintance's son was being interrogated.

That was good. Tari hadn't given anything away.

"Verrat," Pel said in greeting. He knew how haggard and stressed he looked; at least he didn't have to fake that. "I need to talk to Roselin. It's about my son."

"Again?" Verrat asked, not unsympathetic. "I don't know that she'll think much of having you show up a second time in her shift. It's almost over—maybe you should try your luck with Levrier instead. He's on next."

He shook his head. It was tempting to wait, try a fresh face, but Levrier was a hardass and Roselin, at least, was probably a little shaken up. She'd been the one to deliver the bad news, and had seen him 'fail' to get through to Bruant earlier that night. It would be the end of a long, rough shift, and he stood better chances she'd get sloppy.

"It needs to be now. She wouldn't want to wait to hear this," he said.

Verrat watched him for a few moments, then shrugged. "I can try, but don't get your hopes up, Stone."

"It's important," Pel stressed, but Verrat just shrugged again and shut the window.

It took several long minutes before anyone came back. Pel didn't fool himself that nobody was watching, even if he couldn't see them, so he refused to shift his weight to try to salve his aching feet. It was unlikely they'd recognize it for what it was, but he didn't dare give it away, just in case.

Anything could ruin this, right now.

Finally, the window slid open again. Roselin looked tired, strained. "You're going to have to leave, Pelerin."

"I have information," he said. "You'll want this."

"Well? Go on."

"I need to come in," he said, his urgency also unfaked. "I need to show you. The proof is important, and you need to *see* it. Take me to Bruant's room."

Roselin's face grew tighter. "A second time?"

"It's fine," he said, leaning up closer to the window. "This information will change everything. Shit, if you're trying to hide him from me because you've roughed him up, I don't care. You'll see why it doesn't matter what you've done to him."

"If you're planning some kind of rescue—"

Pel let out a shaky laugh. *Too close to home.* "No. I don't need to rescue my son anymore. That's not my son. I'll show you."

For a long moment, he didn't think it would work. And then the door unlatched and Roselin held it for him. "Be quick about it," she said shortly. "Exactly as before. You can enter the cell. I'll guard the door. Show me whatever. If this really does change everything, you'll be rewarded. If it doesn't... I'll mark it down. You won't be able to come in again and you can't work with us any more, Pelerin. Not if you're playing with us here."

"Trust me." He tried to keep his hands from shaking. "You've trusted me these fourteen years, Roselin, and I've never led you astray. Trust me now."

She gave him a hard look, but he could tell from the way she'd relaxed her shoulders that it had worked. Relenting, she turned to lead the way down the hall. Pel had been here before, and it wasn't an unfamiliar path, but he let himself think about how it must have been for the victims, cold stone and fear and pain and the awareness they'd never leave.

How many false confessions did the Inquisition get just because their victims knew there was no way out and just wanted the agony to end?

He felt sick. *Never again, he promised himself. Never.*

"Here," Roselin said. She detached the seal on the door handle, holding it in her hand as she unlocked it and gestured Pel in ahead of her.

Tari looked up as Pel entered, eyes widening in

shock and fear.

For a moment, his heart almost stopped. The cubant looked so perfectly like Bruant that the last few hours briefly seemed unreal, the rescue a failure, and the horror on "Bruant's" face was something other than Tari thinking the plan had gone awry.

"Dad?" Tari whispered, breaking through Pel's paralysis. "What is it? Why are you back?"

"So," Roselin said from behind him. "What do you have to show me?"

Even though their entire escape had taken place at night, it didn't look like the Inquisition had been resting in trying to get a confession. "Bruant" was sitting stiffly on the stiff cot in the cell and breathing shallowly as if to protect damaged ribs, face discolored, an eye swollen almost closed.

Fuck.

Pel's heart squeezed again. He knew what he had to do, but he didn't like it. Bracing himself, he drew a slow breath in. "Roselin, you have to keep the door unlocked or this won't work."

"Unlocked?" Roselin repeated, suspicious, but didn't move to lock it.

Pel didn't respond. He raised a hand and pointed at Tari. "I have your true name, demon."

Tari's eyes went huge with shock and barely-concealed betrayal. "Dad?" Tari asked again, voice raw. "Please, what are you doing—"

"Don't call me that with my son's voice!" Pel yelled, because that part, at least, he meant. He was exhausted, terrified, sick, and he forced himself to not hide it, showing it to both Tari and Roselin. "Demon, I have your name. *Tarigan.*"

Tari groaned. "No. Pel, don't—"

"Show your true form, demon," Pel demanded. "Since the door is open, you can transform again, can't you? Show the inquisitor your true form, Tarigan! Tarigan, I command you!"

These cells were meant to detain witches, but they'd held demons more than once in their time. If his amulet, in combination with Tari's name, might force a weakened Tari to obey sooner or later, the cells should function the same way.

It just wouldn't be pleasant for either of them.

Tari groaned again, writhing, apparently in genuine pain as their body twisted, horns sprouting, limbs extending oddly, tail winding out behind them. It was a form that Tari had previously carried with pride and power, but now, they seemed vulnerable.

Vulnerable, and really pissed off.

"Fuck you, Pel," Tari spat, rising up on their elbows, entire body shaking with rage as much as weakness. "Fuck you!"

Roselin gaped, recoiling back towards the door frame. "What the—fuck, seriously—a demon—!" It had been years since the inquisition had captured a real demon, as far as Pel knew. Roselin was stunned, unprepared for a revelation of this level.

"It is," Pel said, deliberately cold. "As you can see, you never captured my son at all, just this monster."

Tari let out a low growl, threatening and desperate, crouching on the bed, hair falling over their face. "Pelerin Stone—"

Pel forced himself not to listen, to just look at Roselin. "And if you think *that's* impressive, look *here*." He pointed down.

Roselin's gaze snapped to where he was pointing, lowering her face just in time to meet Pel's fist, rising in a sharp uppercut.

She let out a shout as he hit her nose with a sickening crunch, sending a spray of hot blood across his face. He grabbed the ward out of her hand as she was left reeling, shoving her hard and slamming her out of through the doorway. He flung the ward down the hall after her, trying to get it out of whatever line would keep Tari confined, and spun back, holding a hand out to Tari, palm up.

"Come on, Tari!"

"Wh—"

"The door's open!"

For a moment, he didn't think Tari was going to understand, still shocked and betrayed. His heart sank. They stared back at him, blue eyes wild and unseeing, teeth bared, shoulders hunched.

Roselin was rolling on the floor, stunned and with her nose broken, but she was a fighter. She would be on her feet shortly, and he was no match for her in a fair fight, not unarmed and tired and without the element of surprise on his side. Others, too, would doubtlessly be on their way already, drawn by Roselin's yell. They only had seconds.

He held out both hands to Tari, desperate, and cried out, "Tari, please!"

Tari launched off the bed, hooves clattering on stone as they ran across the room, charging at Pel. He drew a sharp breath, but didn't withdraw, keeping his arms out as Tari reached toward him—and grabbed his hands, clasping on tight. Tari's momentum slammed him out of the cell and into the hallway, pressed to the wall with Tari against him. Tari pressed close, sucking a deep relieved breath in, and Pel took advantage of it to kiss them.

He kissed them hard, desperately, knowing how little time he had for this, and poured all his exhausted stores of desire into them. He thought of everything arousing that he could in that short, frantic time, trying to reach as deeply into himself as possible and find the desire there. All the things he'd wanted to do with them, that night Tari had stopped him. All those nights of loneliness where he didn't pursue pleasure with anyone else. The thrill of this moment, of escaping together, how much he wanted them even now. Even Phalene—that first night together on the roof, their *many* nights together in the time they'd had. He thought about all those moments, trying to push them into Tari.

And Tari groaned, accepting that offering and drinking deep. An almost sickeningly strong rush of arousal poured through him, his cock getting hard at once. Tari was taking more than he was giving, forcing his arousal to deepen so they could swallow it down, but Pel allowed it.

And then their lips parted. Grinning and a little wild-eyed, Tari breathed against his mouth, "Hold on."

"Wha—"

"*Hold on*," they repeated, twisting in his grip so that their back was against his front. The sound of a sword being drawn made his attention snap back to the moment; he could see, over Tari's shoulder, that the guards had arrived. Rosalin was being helped to her feet by one even as she began to draw her blade, but several other were approaching, fully armored and closing in.

Pel wished he'd brought a weapon. He'd never have been allowed to bring it in, but anything had to be better than having it end like this. He drew a sharp breath, bracing himself for their charge—and as he did, Tari transformed.

Their shape billowed under him, rising, becoming bigger and bigger. He held onto a neck that thickened to waist width, then more, straining the width of his arms as he was lifted off the floor. It was dizzying, especially in the aftermath of his energy being taken, and he squeezed his eyes shut, scrambling with his legs to find a purchase on the wide, furred sides under him, finding them against the joint between that and leathery wings.

The manticore under him roared, and he opened his eyes as Tari bounded through the halls, moving fast, swiping guards aside until they broke free of the front door and those strong wings began to beat, launching them into the air.

"Crossbows," he gasped, more out of fear than from actually spotting any—but Tari was moving fast, *too* fast, inhumanly so, climbing rapidly. And then, clinging hard and trying not to look down, he yelled accusingly, "Kip said you could only transform into things humans fantasized about!"

The leonine sides under him vibrated for a moment in a low growled laugh. "Sweetheart," Tari said, voice like thunder, "you have a real shock coming to you about what some people like."

I'm just... not going to think about that. "So am I 'sweetheart' again?"

"Looks like you are," Tari said, and circled higher quickly enough that Pel had to shut up to keep the air from being sucked out of his lungs.

Chapter Ten

We've done it, he thought in numb shock, eyes squinted shut against the rush of wind. There was no way the Inquisition could be following them. They'd moved quickly and were far past the city already.

Tari flew above the river, following his directions, but landed before they reached camp. At least, he reassured himself, they had traveled a good way down the path that had taken Pel and the other hours to walk. Tari transformed as soon as Pel was off their back, returning to their intercubus form, though this time wearing their usual clothes rather than Bruant's.

They didn't look good.

Tari was wheezing softly with effort, a strained sound to their breath as they stumbled down the river bank to the water, kneeling there and splashing their face.

Pel watched from a grassy patch just beyond the bank, uncertain for a moment of what to do or say. He waited while Tari refreshed, then rose to walk over to them again, holding out a hand.

"Hey, uh," he said awkwardly. "I'm sorry."

Pel wasn't sure how an apology like that would be taken. It was short and simple but covered, he felt, more ground than having to list specifics. *Sorry that you ended up stuck there. Sorry that you got hurt. Sorry I had to betray you and force you to violently change forms under immense pain and complete exposure.*

The basics.

A vast range of expressions flickered across Tari's face: Annoyance, resignation, amusement. Resignation again. Finally, Tari simply shrugged, dredging up a faint smile. "I can't say I much like an entire inquisitorial force knowing my name," they said, "but I've given it out freely enough before. I've really forgotten what it's like to have that be a threat. It's much less of one when you're living places where folks who try to bind demons would rapidly find themselves overpowered by other demons not wanting them to get cocky."

"I can't imagine any of us wanting to go back to Dolana any time soon," Pel said, finding to his relief that the thought didn't sting as much anymore.

He let his hand drop.

Tari watched the motion with a strange look on their face, leaving Pel to wonder if he'd withdrawn too quickly for Tari to have decided what to do. "No, not any time soon," they said. "*You* could have, though. If you'd truly sold me out while I was trapped, you could have freed Bruant from their suspicion. Anything he'd been caught doing could have been the work of a transformed demon. Then the two of you could have gone back to your normal lives."

Pel swallowed. It had occurred to him when Tari had first brought up the plan. "Sure," he said. "But what would have happened to you, then? Or even Kip? Bruant seems pretty..." he hesitated over the word to use, "*taken* with him. What kind of room would there be for you two in a life like that?"

"No room at all," Tari said quietly. "Just like that city wants. Just like you wanted."

"Maybe," Pel said, "I want more in my life than that

now."

He held out his hand again, and this time, Tari took it.

They sank down on the grass by the river. It was, at least, softer than the stone-covered riverbank. He did wish there was a bed, if they were going to do this. *But honestly, if one were available, I'd probably fall asleep before I could do anything else.*

After all they'd been through, he was *not* going to let that happen.

Groaning before their mouths even touched, he kissed Tari, sliding fingers into their hair and pressing his tongue between their lips, tasting exhaustion and pain and desire. Tari made a soft sound, tongue twining with his before nipping it, rough—drawing blood with sharp teeth.

Pel gasped, startled and a little shocked with the spark of pain. Tari didn't need blood, surely—but when he drew back from the kiss to look at them, nose-to-nose, he caught them looking nearly as dazed and hazy as he was sure he did. Tari let out a soft, needy sound as the kiss broke, swaying back forward. The sound shot through Pel in a spike of arousal.

Maybe it didn't matter if Tari *needed* blood, strictly speaking. They obviously wanted to taste it. *That's fine, isn't it? This much isn't enough to hurt.*

He crushed his mouth to Tari's again, pressing his bloodied tongue back into their mouth.

Tari moaned around it, swallowing a mouthful as they pressed closer, kissing him frantically. They ate at each other's mouths, grabbing whatever they could touch—waist, hips, shoulders, hair. He found himself changing his grip almost helplessly, as though he couldn't touch enough all at once, hands desperate to feel what he'd been denying them, and finally finding it.

He broke the kiss again just long enough for them both to suck a quick breath before leaning back in, arms wrapping around Tari and *pulling*. He sank back under their weight as Tari pressed him into the grass, grinding against him with a sinuous movement, face tight with pleasure. Arching under it, Pel pushed into the touch, breaking the kiss to nip along their jaw to their neck. The mark from before was gone, but it didn't matter; he sucked another one into its place, biting and pulling at the flesh there. It wasn't possession, he thought—just wanting, however briefly, to leave his mark on them.

"Tari..." he murmured, satisfied, as he drew back to gaze up at them. He felt like there was so much more he wanted to say, but he couldn't get his jumbled thoughts in order. The only thing he could really think was, *This is important*, and he felt that at the end of a long day of demons and betrayal and inquisitions, that might just be too strange to say.

Tari let out a short, rough sound, looking down at him with their lips curved. "You might as well use my real name now," they breathed. "So long as you don't mean to bind me to it this time." In one smooth movement, they grabbed the bottom of their shirt and pulled it over their head without undoing half the buttons. Somehow, it didn't get caught on their horns, and given that they'd created the clothes on their own body, he could only assume shapeshifting was involved in that feat.

He had no complaints about the result. "Tarigan," he murmured obediently, sliding his hands up from their waist, cupping their small breasts, rubbing the rough edges of his thumbs over their nipples and making them shudder. Their mouth had fallen open a little and their brows were furrowed, distracted by the sensation, and he found he was really, really taken with the expression.

"You're... really cute." He'd found his words, finally, and abruptly wished that he hadn't. It came out unbidden and he felt himself flush, waiting to be teased.

Startled, Tari snorted a laugh, then bent over him again to kiss him, fierce and quick and heated. "Is that what I am?" they asked, more playful than offended, smirking at him.

"You're—" Pel groaned as Tari's fingers made quick work of the buttons on his shirt, opening it and then running over his chest, finding his nipples and pinching in return. He let out another low noise, arching up as a new wave of heat rushed through him. "I forget. Shit. I'm tired."

"You were praising me," Tari reminded him, but drew back reluctantly, looking down at him with their hands spread on his chest. "Are you sure you want to—?"

Suddenly moved by the thoughtfulness, he touched their cheek. "I'm sure," he said after a long moment. He'd spent a long time trying to guess what other people might want from him, what he could do for them, then doing it regardless of the truth. Bruant had struggled against that, and Phalene—Phalene wasn't even alive to have a say.

She'd made her own choices, and had followed her heart, wherever that had led her. It was probably about time he tried to do the same.

"I'm very sure," he told Tari, and found that he

meant it. "It's... fine. I'm fine. Come here?"

Their expression gentled, and for a moment they leaned their cheek into his palm. And then they *grinned*, pure mischief, eyes glittering as they rose. Standing over him, they said, "Well, then. Get your pants off." They were doing the same, unfastening their belt and shimmying out.

Pel didn't immediately, not with the view this afforded him. Instead, he watched from the ground, finding his cheeks growing even hotter.

Quite frankly, it was a view well worthy of admiration. For a moment he just stared, gazing at their erection, the softer mound behind. He swallowed. "You're lovely," he said softly, eyes passing over their lean figure, shuddering with another wave of desire. Still, he slowly shuffled backward to get a better image of the whole: tall twisting horns over long wavy hair, narrow shoulders and slim waist, wide hips, the oddly-angled legs, a tail winding around their ankles.

A demon, but also just Tari. He acknowledged it, felt it settle, as though something clicked into place and fit there, comfortable and right.

Tari watched him with heavy eyelids. They gave him a moment, waited until he'd lifted his gaze back to their eyes, then smiled. "Glad you like what you see," they drawled. "Now. Are you going to get your pants off or am I going to have to get them off you?"

"I think you're going to have to get them off," he said, so hard that it might be difficult, but hoping that Tari *would*. He found himself grinning at the delighted, hungry look the idea put on their face.

Laughing, Pel grabbed two handfuls of grass as Tari dropped to their knees and crawled up him, dragging their body against his. Their cock settled between his legs as Tari braced over him, leaning down for another kiss. He let out a shudder, arching up to grind again.

But he didn't get a chance, letting out a rush of breath as Tari abruptly flipped him. The grass in his hands was pulled out and loose as he scrabbled for another handhold while Tari got a hand on his waistband, dragging his pants off.

He lay on his front, drawing several quick breaths before Tari was back, leaning down against him, long hair trailing against his skin. "Turn over again," they murmured. "I want to kiss you some more."

He caught his breath, surprised by the almost romantic tone in their voice but liking it, enjoying the flush of warmth and the swell of affection in his chest, filling something too-long kept empty.

I'd missed that, too.

He rolled over, leaning up into the kiss, hands roaming down Tari's back. He found the place where their tail sprouted and curled his fingers around it, curious, letting out a soft chuckle when Tari twisted a little, squirming. "Ticklish?" he managed to ask, grinning.

"Not the word I'd use," Tari said, grinning back.

So he did it again, more firmly.

Tari arched, pleased, straddling his chest to make that easier for him. He shuddered at the intense arousal that washed over him at the way that felt—and felt a spike of anxiety rise, sudden. "I'm tired," he warned, with deep reluctance. "I don't know how much I can..."

"Whatever you can give, I'll take," Tari said, smirking. "Besides, we've got quite a long trip ahead of us. We can do whatever we like, whenever we like."

"A trip with my *son*," Pel protested, leaning back to look up at them.

Tari snort-laughed again, indelicate. "Don't think he won't be sneaking off for privacy too," they said. "We'll find moments to seize. Now, you've got me in this position—what do you want to do with me?"

Pel shuddered hard, then slid his hands up to draw Tari up higher, closer. Their cock rubbed against his lips and he touched the tip of his tongue to it, wetting his mouth and groaning at the taste.

"Pel..." Tari's mouth dropped open slightly, horizontal pupils flaring wide in a rush. They drew a shuddering breath in, stomach tensing in anticipation.

Good—the thought that he could surprise Tari was surprisingly intoxicating, urging him onward to wrap his lips around the head of their cock and draw them into his mouth. He didn't take them deep—didn't dare to, unpracticed as he was—and they didn't try to make it happen, not moving, just gazing down at him with a hitching breath. Instead, he wrapped his fingers around the base, squeezing it as his other hand slid along Tari's ass until his fingers found their soft, wet opening. He pressed them in, curling gently.

Tari *moaned*, deep and pleased, arching over him and raising their own hands to tweak their nipples as he sucked at the head, twisting his tongue around it, his fingers working in them. He felt almost overcome with need, aching to be touched, but he didn't want to stop to try to take care of himself. He wanted to make them feel good—wanted to take his time exploring.

That indulgence appealed to him so much more right then than any physical pleasure would alone.

It didn't seem to be long at all before Tari planted a hand on the ground beside his head, bent a little and sucking deep breaths. "I want to come," they groaned.

The sound of it, of Tari saying that to him, hit Pel hard. He struggled to take them deeper in his mouth, wanting to feel them, taste them, unable to stop an involuntary, desperately begging sound.

But they pulled away, pressing his fingers deep into them—and pulling their cock out of his mouth. He made a noise of protest, trying to chase it, then let out a helpless cry as Tari came across his face, hot, their body pulsing around his fingers.

For a moment, he just panted for breath, stunned and pleased at the realization he'd made them come. It filled him with an embarrassing, boyish delight as he felt a sticky wetness slide down his cheek slowly, caught in his stubble.

"Good," Tari breathed, eyes bright as they gazed down at him.

Then they pulled back, straddling his waist. Pel groaned aloud as their fingers wrapped around him, shifting helplessly into the touch, wanting, *needing*, desperate. A warm wet heat enveloped him as Tari lowered their hips, pulling him inside them and making him arch up helplessly. He shuddered with the overwhelming wave of need and want and how much he'd missed this, how much he'd missed having someone to hold. "Tari—"

"Touch me, then," they whispered, as though he'd said it aloud. "Hold me."

Drawing a sharp breath in, Pel pulled Tari down against him, gathering them in his arms and holding them as closely as he could in their position. He felt like he must be squeezing them, clinging on, and had a spike of worry about if he might hurt them—but Tari was making low, pleased sounds, and when he realized that, he gave up thinking entirely, overcome by the heat and pressure and his own need, rocking up in frantic, hard strokes, once, twice—

He came so hard and suddenly that he couldn't even choke out a warning, just bit down on Tari's lower lip as he spilled into them, peripherally aware that Tari was still moving, murmuring, flushed and needy.

He'd barely when Tari broke the kiss to moan, *loud*, shuddering and coming a second time. They spilled out over Pel's stomach, panting loudly for breath. For a moment, he was almost dizzy, feeling Tari draw on him in some way, pulling at his spirit the same way they were pulling at his body with that sucking pressure.

And then he was done, wrung out of pleasure, head dropping back as he sucked great gasps of air. Tari sat back on his hips with a content sound, licking their lips, satisfaction spread across their features—

—and then Tari was shaking him awake. He'd dozed off instantly, he realized groggily, and shook himself. "How long—"

"Not long," Tari said. "Sorry, I know you need to sleep."

He blinked rapidly, trying to will his vision to clear. "No, it's—it's good," he said. The words came out with a quiet sound of wonder, and he flushed a little at it, both embarrassed and pleased.

Tari smiled at him, putting a hand over his. "It's good," they agreed gently. "Come on, get up. You can rest soon, but not here."

That was like a bucket of cold water, washing away his gentle contentment. "Why, are we in danger?"

"Not that I know of," Tari said, smiling. "But your son's only a twenty-minute walk from here, so I thought you might want to go a bit further before sleeping." They walked back down the river bank, sitting by the edge to clean up.

Pel blinked, then went scarlet, stumbling down to join them, splashing himself, scrubbing at his sticky face. *No, I was wrong. Actual cold water is a significantly worse wake-up.* He endured it as best he could. "But then—why did we stop here?"

Tari turned and gave him the most exaggeratedly patient expression he'd ever seen in his life.

"Oh," he said.

They snickered. "Yeah," they said. "Also, I didn't feel up to walking into an encampment while your son and his familiar were making love. In the state I was in, I'd pretty much have to feed on it." They smirked at Pel. "Thought you might dislike that about as much as you'd dislike startling them in the middle of things."

Pel made a disgruntled noise. It wasn't exactly a surprise to hear, but he'd sort of wanted to avoid thinking about it fully until he'd had a night of sleep, and maybe hadn't just upended his entire life. "So they're—*together* together."

"What did you *think* their 'love' meant?" Tari gave him an amused look, then rose, going back to where they'd discarded their clothes and pulling them on. Again, Pel had a strange feeling it was more like reabsorbing matter than anything normal. There had been buttons left done up that didn't seem to need to be undone as Tari dressed again. "Were you writing it off as some kind of weird, magician-familiar bond, nothing you could relate to?"

"Mostly I hadn't let myself think about him and his *cat*," Pel admitted as he began to dress as well, with a more human lack of efficiency.

Tari lifted a brow. "Is it a problem?"

"No," Pel said, and found that he meant it. "As long as he's happy."

~~*

They found the encampment quickly, just as Tari had promised. Bruant was fast asleep on the ground, covered by a single thin blanket, while Kip was awake in his arms, alert and clearly on guard. His head shot up over the curve of Bruant's shoulder when the two of them walked up, and his eyes grew huge with surprise and joy.

Pel opened his mouth to say something, but Tari shushed them both, then mimed sleeping, pointing at Bruant. Kip hesitated, then lay back down, visibly vibrating with excitement but obediently staying quiet to let Bruant rest.

"Your turn now," Tari whispered to Pel, who was, in fact, already heading for where Kip had put his own pack, digging through it to pull his own blanket out.

"Join me?" Pel whispered back, a little embarrassed but valiantly soldiering past it. Without waiting for their answer, he found a patch of grassy ground that seemed tolerably soft. *So long as my bed isn't directly on a mound of fire ants, I'm pretty sure nothing could stop me from sleeping at this point.*

They shrugged. "Why not?" they sighed, almost rueful. "I could use some rest too. It's been a long week."

Pel lifted the blanket and held it up until Tari crawled in with him, flopping down and draping an arm over him, cuddling up. Never mind the sunlight, the strangeness of sleeping outside with company, or anything else—Pel was asleep again before he could even tuck the blanket around them.

Bruant tackled him awake a few hours later. "Dad," Bruant sobbed, "you made it. And you brought Tari—"

"Oof," Tari groaned. "Easy there, kiddo, that was my stomach."

Dazed, Pel lifted an arm and wrapped it around Bruant. "I'm glad you two are still okay. We got out fine. No harm done."

"Do you know how fucking scared I was?" Bruant demanded, voice cracking. "Don't just play it off like that..." He sat back, shaking and somewhere between angry and terrified, cheeks wet and eyes bloodshot.

No wonder, Pel thought. Bruant knew better than any of them what it was like to be taken by the Inquisition, and Pel had gone and walked right back in there.

"Yeah," Pel said. "I know." Which nowhere near addressed his thoughts or feelings, but, as always, he seemed to have trouble finding the words to give his son. He added, "I mean, I *know*."

Bruant hesitated, then shuffled back on his knees. "We should get moving again," he said. He drew a deep breath, rubbing his face with his hands, then managed a smile. "If you're up to it. Kip says he hasn't noticed any pursuit, and maybe they won't follow us out this far, but I don't want to risk it. Not now that we're all finally safe."

Pel groaned. "I'm up to it, sure. Stiff from sleeping on the ground, but nothing worse." He turned to Tari. "You're the one who knows the way around here, so it's in your hands. Where are we going exactly? Still following the river?"

"To the main road, at least," Tari said. They'd risen from where they were lying, and were stretching—apparently checking how well their ribs still worked, between the Inquisition and Bruant's enthusiasm. Pleased, they grinned. "That's pretty heavily traveled, and by other demons too. We'll be safe there, at least from your city's demon-hunters." They hesitated, then rose, gathering the blanket from over Pel and starting to fold it, a strangely mundane gesture in the hands of a cubant. "After that? Depends on where you want to go."

"You were going to go—" Pel cut himself off. "Oh, shit. Your jewels. We left them back at Orphie's—"

Tari huffed a laugh, light. "I don't give a shit about jewels, Pel. I wish Orphie much joy of them—they're just a good excuse when I'm traveling as a human. And I don't think going on to a city like Levisham is a good idea regardless, not with two humans who've barely seen demons before. Got any family outside of Dolana?"

Pel shook his head. "My parents are both dead," he said. "I had an older sister who left the city. She'd been apprenticing as a blacksmith, and wanted to find a city with better trade routes so she could seek her fortune, but I don't know where she ended up or if she's still alive."

Tari made a face. "Ah. That's rough. My own siblings at least keep contact. What about you, Kip, anywhere you want to go?"

"Wait," Pel interrupted. "*Siblings*? I didn't think demons have those. Kip said you didn't grow up or anything—"

"So what?" Tari was, remarkably enough, visibly flustered, crossing their arms and glaring a little, though there was no heat to the expression. "Sometimes demons hatch together. Sometimes we think that means something to us. Kip, seriously, give an opinion if you have one."

Pel opened his mouth to question that further, but Kip was already talking, snuggling in against Bruant, utterly content and oblivious to—or steadfastly ignoring—their reactions. "Honestly, I don't know what other cities are like," Kip admitted. "But I don't care where we go as long as Bruant's fine with it."

Bruant said, almost defensive, "I don't know either! Don't put this on me, Kip, I can't—I really can't—Tari, you're the one who'd probably know best what'd suit us."

Tari stepped back a few steps, having recovered from their embarrassment like it had never happened. Pel resolved to make it happen again, as soon as possible, as they made a frame of their fingers to encompass the three of them. "A new demon, barely experienced in the world," they noted, taking stock in a pointedly dramatic tone. "A magician partnered to this new demon, who barely has a spell to his name. And an ex-guard who has just started to get over his hatred of demons, due entirely to the help of a friendly passing cubant."

All three of them began to protest their descriptions, talking over each other; Tari held a hand up. Pel forced himself to shut up when the others did, even though he felt his was *especially* unfair after everything that had happened.

"I'm taking you to Potfeld." Tari decided. "It's where I was hatched, and I never stay away for too long. It's a nice place. The citizens are mostly humans, but demons pass through freely all the time. The ruler is Hrahez—Prince Hrahez, that is—and he's really almost stupidly soft. He's got an injunction on keeping demons from doing harm, at least without consent, to humans in his cities. The roads are a bit more dangerous, but given that Kip and I are going with you, you'll be fine."

"So basically," Pel said slowly, starting to smile, "you want to take us to your home. So, do your siblings live there, too?"

"I wouldn't quite put it like—there are things and people I want to check up on, and—" Tari cut themself off, then huffed. Pel wasn't sure it if was his imagination, but they seemed slightly red-faced. "Sure," they said, sulky. "Whatever."

"Bruant?" Pel asked.

Bruant shrugged. "Sounds nice to me," he said softly. "I bet I could learn there. I bet they'd have what I need." He glanced hesitantly at Pel, who smiled at him encouragingly.

"Kip?"

Kip grinned, the tip of his tongue peeking out. "I'll go wherever Bruant goes," he repeated, "but it does sound like a good place to get a start."

A start...

Pel nodded. He took the folded blanket from Tari, who was now holding it like they didn't know what to do with it, and put it in his pack, before slinging it onto his shoulder.

"Then that's settled," he said. He gestured to Tari to lead the way. "Let's go home."

Fin

About the Author

Meredith Katz started writing around the same time she started to walk, a 6 page 'book' called "The Baby Dragon" (spoilers, there was an egg, it hatched, and then there was a baby dragon). She hasn't stopped since, and after many years of writing slash and femslash fanfiction, she is only too excited to share her original fiction. She lives in beautiful BC, Canada with her gorgeous fiancée and adorably nerdy cat.

Tumblr: http://king-of-katz.tumblr.com
Website: https://meredithakatz.wordpress.com

Made in the USA
Lexington, KY
30 September 2017